# Life After Fifty

A NOVEL

Laulie Powell

Copyright © 2023 by Laulie Sue Powell. All rights reserved.

No part of this publication may be reproduced or used in any form or by any means graphic, electronic, or mechanical, including photocopying, recording, taping, or via information and retrieval systems without written permission of the author. This is a work of fiction. Names, characters, businesses, places, events, and incidents are either the products of the author's imagination or are used in a fictitious manner.

979-8-9899302-0-3
979-8-9899302-1-0

Cover image by Wirestock


The opinions or assertions contained herein are those of the author. They are not to be construed as official or reflecting the views of the US Marine Corps.

*In memory of Julia Anne Sweet Powell*

Also by Laulie Powell

*Embrace and Flow*

*Color by Number*

*The Flight Jacket*

*Behind the Curtain*

# Grace

When I was a teenager, I couldn't even imagine what it would be like to be as old as fifty. That idea was like the sun when it was so far below the horizon that its rays were barely visible. But when I was one month beyond my fiftieth birthday, I was forced to reimagine the rest of my life. This is because I'd had a stroke.

Looking back with the wonderful twenty-twenty vision of hindsight, I couldn't help but think that events in my life had combined to cause it: the stress and anxiety of my jobs, the heartache of failed marriages, and the heartbreak of a lost love. But, perhaps it was completely physical: my body's changes as I went through menopause combining with a congenital heart defect, a tiny hole left there when my body was preparing itself to come into this world. I was told this was a common birth defect, appearing in one out of ten people, but I was one of the unfortunate ones in which this small hole had provided the pathway for a blood clot to make its way to my brain. There the infarction damaged my ability to speak, a condition called aphasia, and damaged my short-term memory. Of course, it could have been so much worse, but having been a lawyer, my ability to call up the right words at the right time and retain information in my memory defined who

I was in this world and gave me a sense of standing. Overnight, those gifts were gone, never to be recovered.

Since the time of my rebirth, as I came to call it, I have been a different person because I have a different version of my brain. For as my mind slowly but surely started to heal itself, I was forced to realize I had changed forever. For one thing, I had become more of a listener than a talker. In my case, aphasia impaired my ability to call up the nouns I wanted to use to express myself. When I was tired or hadn't slept well, it took me longer to come up with words, and sometimes the words were close to what I wanted to express but not quite right. And my short-term memory was now a sieve, affecting my ability to retain information like phone numbers, directions, and the types of things an undamaged memory can hold on to for a short while. But the worst aspect of my memory loss was my inability to remember if I had told someone something or not. This one effect seemed to age my mind immeasurably. I adopted a famous saying, attributed to many, including Abraham Lincoln, as an example of how to behave with people: "Tis better to be silent and be thought a fool, than to speak and remove all doubt." I mourned the loss of my excellent memory and the ease of speaking, the right words no longer automatically coming to my lips without any conscious thought.

As a listener who wasn't waiting to speak, I became an observer. It was like I had pulled out of fast-moving traffic, parked, turned off the car, and just sat there, watching the world go by. The positive aspect of my new self was that I was finally fully mature. I no longer looked at the world from my perspective only but took a broader view. Added to that, I was no longer interested in drinking alcohol. Perhaps I quit drinking because alcohol dulled my senses, and I didn't have as much in the way of senses to dull now. My rose-colored glasses were broken by the stroke, and I saw the world in the bright light of a sun-drenched day. This stark reality forced me to examine who I used to be.

I had thought of myself as this idealistic do-gooder, with a vision of myself as a smart person who had decided early on in her life that she wanted to be a criminal defense attorney. I took literally the legal presumption that a person was innocent until proven guilty. The reality of the true nature of my clients was that some stole, robbed, maimed, and killed. Some were drug abusers, alcohol abusers, women abusers, child abusers, and psychopaths. Some had never had a chance at a decent life, raised in abject poverty, and been victims of crimes before becoming the perpetrators themselves. Seeing the same minor criminals come and go through the court system, as if through a revolving door, and seeing the people who committed serious felonies going to state prison to become institutionalized beat me down and wore away at my idealism, slowly but surely.

The Marine Corps was my ticket to get back on the idealism train, and I jumped aboard without looking back. The Marine Corps is steeped in heroic ideals and imbued with high-sounding qualities like honor, courage, and commitment, but there was also an understanding that by joining it, I would undertake a selfless devotion to duty. Its training cut away the fluff, made me tough physically, and held me to a high standard of behavior. As a lawyer, I was on the periphery of the Corps' organizational theory, realizing that many of the people who joined the Corps wanted and needed a place where they could act out their fantasies of kicking ass and taking names. When I had finally survived Officer Candidate School and The Basic School, I was physically stronger and mentally sharper and a part of an organization that was trained to kill others, albeit only at the pleasure of the president of the United States. For the years of my thirties and forties, I was under the impression, perhaps because of my training, that I was contributing to a greater good, without ever defining what that was exactly due to the difficulties and stress of the jobs I held.

So, I was shocked at fifty to wake up to the realization of how selfish and self-absorbed I had been. Sure, I had on the surface pursued an idealistic and selfless career, but below the surface, I had been all about myself. I could see no tangible way that I had contributed to the elusive greater good, something I had allegedly dedicated my life to. I found myself struggling with the idea that, for all intents and purposes, my life was over, and I went about my days trying to maintain a positive attitude about having recovered my health with enough money to support myself. Yet I was constantly fighting back the idea that I was just going through the motions of living without actually doing it.

In early spring of 2018, I was speeding along Highway 301, in the backseat of my realtor's SUV, taking in the North Florida landscape, a part of the world I had not seen for over thirty years. Beyond the grassy side of the road, scattered with the litter of aluminum cans and other things people had tossed out the windows, I studied the flora: tall pine trees scattered among water and laurel oaks, small scrub magnolia trees, palmettos, and the ubiquitous kudzu vines, growing up the trees. Beyond the trees, there were concrete electric poles going off into the distance in two directions. I saw a few huge dark-pink azaleas in bloom, a splash of bright color against the drab green-and-brown backdrop, as well as wildflowers in the road median. This landscape was only broken by the billboards advertising personal injury law firms and wonders to be found on the road ahead, like barbeque and burger places.

I wondered if William Bartram, a botanist and traveler to North Florida in the late 1700s, would recognize anything.

Bartram published his book in 1791, filling it with the plants, wildlife, and scenes of North Florida along the St. Johns River and over to Tallahassee and back. The antique style of his prose lent his descriptions a vivid yet fairy-tale quality. Admittedly, there was little, if anything, of fairy tale quality along this road.

Nothing had changed in the look of the landscape, but seeing a speed limit sign for forty-five miles per hour, I knew the town of Lawtey couldn't be far ahead. I moved up on my seat to talk to my realtor, Annie, who was driving.

—You better slow down a little. The cops around here make their living giving out tickets to people going over the posted speed limit.

—Thanks. Good to have some local scoop, Annie said, smiling at me in the rear view mirror.

—Did you know, I said, that this four-lane highway was advertised in the 1950s as the quickest route from New York to Florida? One of the first roads built where people could drive directly to Tampa. I'm thinking forty-five miles per hour was normal for back then.

—I've never traveled on it before, Annie said.

Her husband, Jeff, a big, blond Canadian, with an "I've never met a stranger" way about him, chimed in.

—I haven't either, he said. Always take I-95 or I-75, depending on if we're going southeast or southwest.

—That's perfectly understandable, I said, turning my head to look at him, considering you can get where ever it is you're going a lot faster. But, if you want to take your time, this route is more leisurely and . . . colorful, I'd guess you'd say. I smiled at him, and he grinned back.

We slowed down as we drove through Lawtey. It was marked by gas stations, drive-through places for a quick bite to eat, and several blocks of one-story businesses. Between Lawtey and the next town, Starke, the roadway was marked by a jumbled array of different-sized signs announcing that we were coming upon a mecca of fruit and vegetable stands. These three-sided wooden stalls each carried the end of the winter season's citrus fruits, like tangerines, grapefruits, and navel oranges. Some stands featured strawberries that looked to have been grown in the fields directly to the rear of the stands. There were still pecans for sale, harvested from nearby trees.

And, there was the occasional vintage motel. I wasn't sure if the buildings I remembered from childhood were the same ones I caught glimpses of as we passed. It was hard to tell. They were all one story, spread out in a row, with less than one dozen rooms. The names had changed—no longer names like Alligator Inn or Orange Blossom Motel. They were now chain motels, the names indicating they were inexpensive places to spend the night.

But, another part of my mind was thinking about how I found myself on my way to this part of the state to look at houses. After the first of the year, I had woken up one morning and decided to sell my house in Jacksonville and move out of the city. It wasn't a snap decision but one which my mind had been considering ever since I had moved back there a decade earlier. There had always been a tiny nagging pull at the back of my mind, a niggling feeling that I couldn't seem to ignore. I believed it was because I hadn't yet found a place that felt like home. As I had gotten older, I had come to believe that home is the place that centers and grounds a person, not just physically but emotionally as well. Jacksonville was just a holding place, close to my sisters, and over the last ten years, that had been enough.

Six months earlier, I had begun looking at Zillow in the evenings before bedtime as a way to do something while not really doing anything. I had started looking at houses outside of Pensacola and the towns along the Gulf Coast. But although those areas were not yet densely populated, they were quickly growing, and I dreamed of more space. Then I had, on a whim, taken a look at the houses in the place we were on our way to now. From the pictures of the houses and surrounding areas, it seemed little changed from when I had been there on the weekends and summer vacations as a girl. And, there were properties for sale on lakes with prices I could actually afford. I suppose that's when I began to formulate the thought, bubbling to the top of my mind, to move there.

On a Saturday afternoon in late February, I called Annie on the phone, then walked across the street to talk to her. She listened to me as I told her I was interested in putting my house up for sale and wanted her help. I smiled, watching Annie talking animatedly to her husband, and wondered how much of her nonstop chatter Jeff actually heard. She was well-suited to her chosen profession: upbeat, industrious, well-informed, technologically savvy, well-coiffed, and tastefully dressed. She had been interested in making sure that whoever bought my house was someone who she could live with as a neighbor.

Two days later, while I was in the process of getting the interior of my house ready to photograph for the MLS and before the "for sale" sign went up in the front yard, she called me to see if she could show the house to someone.

—Sure, I said, but you know, it looks really lived-in right now.

—It's not a problem. I've seen the inside of your house.

—Okay, then. What time?

—Two o'clock.

—I guess I'll take the dogs for a nice long walk. Will you call me when you're done showing it?

—Of course, Jules! You know, I've been showing houses to this young woman for a couple of weekends. She's really interested in seeing your house. And, if nothing else, it will give us an idea of what we might need to do to get it ready for the market.

—Sounds good, I said. I figured this would be only the first of many showings.

That afternoon, Annie called me while I was still walking my dogs.

—You're done, already? I said.

—Yes! Annie said, excitedly. Where are you?

—Boone Park . . . Why?

—Well, when you get home, don't go anywhere. I'm going to bring an offer over for you . . . actually, an amazing offer.

—You *are* kidding.

—Nope! she said, laughing. See you soon.

The offer was amazing. So much so, I thought the house would never appraise for that much money. But I had been wrong, and the process for closing on the house moved along without a single issue, with a closing scheduled in a little over a month. I was all of a sudden in the throes of finding a place to live.

We made the turn off of 301 in Starke onto the two-lane highway, County Road 100, and headed toward Keystone Heights.

—Let's look at the houses in Keystone first, then we'll hit the one in Melrose, Annie said to me.

—All right. You know, I never really paid attention to the lake houses on Geneva. As a kid, I was so focused on getting to our lake place.

—Well, Jeff said, turning around to look at me, I've never really had a reason to come through here before. It *is* definitely rural.

—It is, which is sort of amazing, I said. It hasn't changed very much. It's surprising, in a way. Jax hasn't really expanded in this direction yet.

—And all the lakes, Jeff said. There are dozens of them. I

checked out the map of the area last night. I had no idea.

—Well, this part of the state sits on top of the Florida aquifer, I said. A couple of the lakes, like Lake Geneva and another big lake called Lake Brooklyn actually directly feed it. When it rains the water goes directly from the lakes down to the aquifer. But from the pictures on Zillow, it looks like the lakes have gone down a lot from when I was a kid. I think it's a combination of the dry weather Florida has experienced for the last ten years or so, all the sand mining in this area, and the demands on the aquifer from the population growth.

He looked at me questioningly.

—I know . . . Leaving our pretty little neighborhood seems crazy, I said, shaking my head, but, I don't know, I feel like this area of the state is calling to me.

—Well, if nothing else, this is a really nice drive, he said. Much prettier than I imagined. Old Florida, I guess you'd call it, with all the big trees.

—Pretty much, I said, nodding at him.

The two houses I was scheduled to look at on Lake Geneva were in Keystone Heights. As we drove through the town's quaint little four-block downtown area, with a gas station, small business storefronts, and the city hall, I spotted Mallard's. I couldn't believe it was still there, but instead of a five and dime variety store, it was a UPS drop-off and supply depot. The building was small, but it loomed large in my memory as a place to get a nickel's worth of candy. I remembered walking down the sidewalk with my father and Cora, my younger sister by two years, on our way to the magic of Mallard's, such a happy memory from childhood.

I knew that this small town and its houses along the lake were established by a land developer from Pennsylvania in the 1920s. The community was named Keystone Heights for his home state. It had soon become a popular destination for summer vacations, with a large, stately hotel and a pier on the waterfront of Lake Geneva. The hotel was gone and the original pier wiped out by a hurricane in the 1940s. But, as we made the turn onto Lakefront Drive, off to my right I could see the beach and a modern pier. I thought they looked well-kept, although I could see water hyacinths covering a good bit of the waterfront. Most of the early and mid-twentieth-century waterfront houses looked well-kept, too. Huge live oak trees dotted the street, the houses set back from the road, with white and pink azaleas and lavender-colored hydrangeas shaded by the thick cover of the trees.

The first house looked promising from the outside, and the inside had been remodeled, but the view out to the lake, I thought, was just sad. The lake water had receded so much that it looked like only a distant mirage. The second house, on the same street a few houses away, looked much the same but with the disadvantage of the view of the yard next door, a yard filled with junk, including an old car up on concrete blocks, an old fishing boat, and a rusted washing machine.

I caught Annie's eye, behind the back of the sellers' realtor who had met us at the houses, shaking my head and mouthing, *No way!*

She and the sellers' realtor exchanged business cards while Jeff and I got back in the SUV.

—Jesus! I said, I don't understand it. How can they stand having all that junk in their yard? I'd have to put up a ten-foot fence all the way down the property line so that I wouldn't have to look at it.

—Like I said, Jeff said, grinning, it's definitely rural.

—Rural zoning doesn't give people the right to live like pigs. I mean, where is their pride? I said, disgusted. The people who established this community are probably turning in their graves.

Annie got in the car.

—On to Melrose, folks! she said. She looked back at me. We can't expect to find the perfect house on the very first outing. You've got plenty of time to find a house. Okay?

—I know, I said, and it's good to have a reality check. I knew the lakes had taken a hit from the lack of adequate rainfall, and you can never underestimate the progress of time. But the reality of seeing Lake Geneva's recession so far out was a shock.

Annie and Jeff just nodded.

—Well, I'm curious to see what the next lake's waterfront looks like, Annie said.

—Me, too. I said.

In less than five minutes, we turned onto State Road 214, and I saw that there was still a gas station on the corner, a modern Shell station, with a large neon sign above the door of the adjacent convenience store.

—That gas station, I said, pointing at it, is still called The Gizmo!

—Gizmo? Jeff said. What does that mean?

—It's a bygone expression, a slang word, for things you don't know the name of. It's where my dad came to get gas for the boat and sometimes for Cokes and ice cream, summer necessities.

Seeing the place brought back a snippet of a memory: going there with my father and seeing the old man, who ran the place, behind the counter, remembering how much he scared me. He was stooped, unsmiling, and sort of smelly, like dirty laundry that had been forgotten and left in a dark closet. But, in examining this memory now with a lifetime of experience, I decided that he had just been beat down by a hard life.

We took in the scenery as we followed the winding, two-lane road, past a large pasture with a heard of grazing cows, past wooded roadsides, mobile homes, and small houses.

As we turned off the paved road onto a sand-and-gravel road,

Annie slowed down, creeping along, avoiding the potholes.

—The address is right up here, she said, as we came upon a sand lane, leading up to a small brick-and-stone house, with huge live oak trees shading it. Beyond the house, I saw the lake where I had spent so much time as a girl.

When we pulled up to the house, a small, frail-looking woman came out into the carport, followed by an equally aged pit bull. As we all got out of the car, my past flooded back: the sound of a boat motor out on the lake, the ever-so-light feel of the wind, stirring the long strands of Spanish moss in the surrounding trees, and the call of a red-tailed hawk. I looked up as I heard it, and caught a glimpse of it above the tops of the trees.

I found myself smiling as the woman introduced herself and her dog, Ruby.

—Do you mind if I walk down to the lake first, before I take a look at the house? I asked her.

—No, go right ahead, but watch where you're walking. I don't get down there much anymore, but Ruby does.

—I won't be a minute.

—I'll join you, Jeff said. Let me just go get my camera out of the car.

Annie turned to the woman.

—You want to show me the house? The woman nodded, calling Ruby to follow her.

Jeff and I started for the lake, walking through mid-calf-length grass, sidestepping Ruby's droppings. *The front of the property had once been a manicured lawn,* I thought. It was primarily St. Augustine grass. There was also long-neglected lawn furniture, along with a downed water oak, looking like some big giant had just yanked it out of the ground and laid it on its side. About five feet from the water were huge cypress trees, their knobby trunks meant for living in the water, now dry and sun-bleached. Some sort of thick lawn grass had grown into the water, going out a good twenty feet. It wasn't saw grass, I knew, the plant that had defined the lake when I was a girl. To my left, I saw the waterfront next door was clear of grass, the sun glinting off the clear water, the yellow sand bottom reflecting a golden glow with minnows everywhere. Looking out across the lake, I saw houses partially obscured by the cypress trees all along the waterfront.

—Looks like a great place to fish, Jeff said.

—My baby sister used to think so, I said, turning to look at him. She loves to fish, but it's not really my thing. She caught a ten-pound bass when she was about fourteen. Right out there, I said, pointing off to the right.

—A bass?

—A largemouth bass. I remember she told me that my dad had given her one lesson in fish cleaning, skinning, and deboning. Then, he told her, "You catch 'em and, if you want to keep 'em, you clean 'em." He was pretty much that way with everything. He showed us once or twice how to do something, then we were on our own.

—Where was your parents' property?

—Over that way. I again pointed off to the right of where we were standing. We didn't pass it on the way here. It's down the road a ways. He sold it right before he died, after my mother died. I was in the Marine Corps at the time, in Bahrain, right before the start of the war with Iraq. And to tell you the truth, I was caught up in my own life. I had no idea.

Turning to the left, I pointed down to the far end of the lake.

—See that undeveloped land?

He turned to look where I pointed, nodding his head.

—That's what most of the lake looked like when I was a kid, although I don't see saw grass anywhere. There used to be saw grass all around the lakefront. Whoever named that plant was a very literal person. Have you ever been cut by saw grass?

—I can't say that I even know what it is.

—It's this tall grass that grows in fresh and brackish waters. The blades of the grass are thin and so sharp they can cut you up, if you brush up against it. You avoid it like the plague, or at least, I did. The cuts are so fine, you can't see them, but you feel them. I don't know for sure, but it must have some sort of toxin on the blades because you'll get an infection if you don't clean your cuts right away.

—Sounds like something you would want to get rid of.

—Yeah, but I can't help thinking it plays some role in keeping the lake's ecosystem in balance. Anyway, I don't see any.

He raised his camera. As I turned to go back up, he continued to snap pictures.

—I'll catch up with you in a minute.

—That's okay. I'll wait on you, I said, closing my eyes and feeling the soft wind on my skin. I heard him coming up behind me, and opened my eyes.

—Do you and Annie still have a booth at the Riverside farmer's market? I said.

—Sure do. It's a good place for me to sell my photographs. I think people will buy these photos of the lake, he said. We'll see... You just never know what people will buy.

As Annie got in the passenger's seat for the drive back to Jacksonville, I waved good-bye to the woman and her dog. Annie turned to me.

—How did the lake look?

—Pretty good. It doesn't seem to have receded as much as Lake Geneva. I'm thinking it's because this lake doesn't directly feed the aquifer. And it's a spring-fed lake. There are spots where cold water flows into it.

—You're a font of info about these lakes! she said.

—No, I'm really not, I said, shaking my head. That's basically everything I know about them.

As we came to the end of the sand-and-gravel road, Jeff looked right and then left: the paved road was empty.

—Let's go left, he said. I want to see your parents' old place.

—Sure, I said. It's right up ahead. See that brick chimney?

—Got it. Look! The gate's open, he said as we came upon the house. Let's have a look. What do you say?

Before I could answer, he had turned into the drive that wound toward the small cottage made of red brick and wood shingles, with its tall chimney on our right, past the citrus trees and the huge Turkey fig tree on the left. Halfway down to the lake, the old wooden swing my father had made was still hanging from the huge live oak tree. I was so surprised that everything looked the same, I half expected to see my father's ghost puttering around in the yard.

As we got out of the car, a man came out of the house.

—Hi there, Jeff said, smiling at him. I'm Jeff. This is my wife, Annie, and this is Jules.

—I'm Jim Walker's daughter, I said, saying the first words that came to mind.

—I'll be! the man said. My name's Tom Wilkinson. Is your dad still alive?

—No, I said, shaking my head. He died a little over sixteen years ago. But, he lived a long life, and he essentially died of old age. I was away in the military when he sold it to you, but he loved this place. He wouldn't have sold it to you if he hadn't felt like you would take care of it.

—That's good to hear, Mr. Wilkinson said, nodding his head. I'm a building contractor by profession, and your dad and I sort of spoke the same language. You want to see the inside of the house? My wife and I don't live here; we live over in Melrose, but we wanted a lake house nearby. I just come over to relax. But, when our kids were younger, we were here every weekend during the summer.

—I'd love to see it! I turned to Annie and Jeff. Do ya'll want to see it?

—Sure! they said in unison, laughing at each other.

Mr. Wilkinson led the way, opening the screen door and then pushing open the heavy front door. The smell of the house—the smell of the cypress wood from which all of the interior beams, walls, and doors were constructed—hit me in the face so hard, it brought tears to my eyes. As we walked through the small house, I could see in my mind's eye the way the house looked the last time I saw it, with boxes stacked along the walls full of things my father had saved from his various projects. I saw unfinished window sills, unfinished walls, and the ceiling with the framing showing, like he was halfway through working on it and had just stopped for a break but never got back to it.

We walked into the back of the house. This had been the original cabin, with a huge fireplace along one wall. Now the entire house had been finished with painted walls and a new kitchen and bathroom. The old jalousie windows, punctured with BB shots in many of them, had been replaced with new energy-efficient windows. But, as I took it all in, I was struck with the feeling that the house was essentially unchanged and had just been given a facelift.

—It looks amazing, I said, turning to look at our host.

—Thanks, he said, smiling and meeting my eyes. My son and I worked on it on the weekends for about six months after my wife and I bought it. I wanted to preserve the structure of the house while updating it. Your sister Helen left us a book of pictures of the house in various stages of construction as your dad was building it.

*Helen!* I thought, darkly.

—How is she doing? he said. She was having some mobility

problems when I last saw her. Don't tell me she died, too.

—She did, a little over nine years ago . . . a heart attack, I said.

—I'm sorry to hear that, he said, like he really meant it.

I just nodded my thanks. I did not want to discuss Helen's lifelong bout with alcohol or her status as the black sheep of the family or the heartache she caused my other two sisters by her alleged pressure on my father to sell this house for the money. I would probably never know the truth of how it happened and Helen's role in it.

When we were again outside, Jeff and Annie got back in their car while I thanked Mr. Wilkinson for the tour.

—No problem, he said. Happy to do it. But wait, before you go. I have something you might want.

He headed off around the house, and I figured he was going to the small storage room on the side of the house that held the pump for the well. I couldn't imagine what he had that he wanted to give to me. A moment later, he walked back around the house with a rectangular piece of cypress wood in his hands, and as he got closer, I recognized it—the sign my father had nailed to the fence at the entrance to the property. Burned into the cypress wood were the words, "The Walkers." He handed it to me.

—At the time, I didn't know why I kept this, he said soberly. Now I do.

Taking it from him, I couldn't stop the tears from coming.

—Thank you . . . thank you so much. I hurriedly wiped away the tears.

He nodded, opening the back door of the SUV for me, closing it, and raising his hand in good-bye.

—What did he give you? said Annie, looking over her shoulder at me and the sign I held in my lap.

—The sign that my dad made. It hung on the fence, near the road.

—Well how about that? Annie said, shaking her head. No one said anything else until we made the left turn back onto Highway 100.

—He's kept that sign for how long? Jeff said.

—Seventeen years. Annie? She turned to look at me. I want to make an offer on the house we just looked at. It can't be just a coincidence that the gate was open, Jeff drove in, and Mr. Wilkinson gave me this—I raised the sign a little from my lap—after keeping it for seventeen years. I know it will make me sound sort of crazy, but I believe this is a sign.

—Yep, looks like a sign to me, Jeff said, grinning.

We all three broke out in laughter.

—As the expression goes, I said, the humor making it easier to voice an insane idea, *this*—and I raised the piece of cypress again—is a sign from cosmic forces at work or something like that. What do you think I should offer for the house?

—Well, said Annie without missing a beat, we could start out below the asking price. The house needs some updating.

—Right, I said, and I noticed that the huge turkey oak tree near the carport looks like it's dying and of course, that downed oak tree in the front, the one that came down in the hurricane two years ago, will have to be removed.

Annie took out her phone and called the seller's realtor.

By the time we got back to Jacksonville, my offer had been accepted.

# It Ain't Me, Babe

Two months later, I was making my way out of chest-high water, pulling behind me an ingenious—and dangerous—long stainless steel tool shaped into a wide vee at the end. The outside edges of the vee held long, sharp, thin blades designed to cut the grass along the edges of freshwater lakes and ponds. When I'd spotted it at the Ace Hardware store in Keystone, I'd been skeptical of its awesome claim "mows down water grass," which was printed on the box in big, block letters. But now as I dropped the tool on the narrow beach of white sand and turned around to look at my work, I was impressed. I had cleared a space of approximately ten by ten feet of growing torpedo grass, the cut grass floating lazily on the surface of the water. I took in the rest of the waterfront, thinking.

My baby sister, Lizzy, upon seeing it, told me its name and what it was: a grass, imported from China about fifty years ago, used to seed fields for feeding cattle. An aggressive grower, it had pointed, torpedo-shaped roots, which helped it crowd out the other grasses, and it was able to survive in up to about eight feet of water. When I had started clearing it out, I was under the mistaken impression I would have it done in no time. But like many things, it was a more complicated project than it had seemed at first glance. I understood now it would involve much more work than just cutting the grass. After cutting it (although I hadn't figured out yet how I was going to cut the grass in the deep water over my head), I would have to get the grass, floating on top of the water, to the shore; give it some time to dry out in the sun; rake it up; and then either burn it or put it in bags to be taken away by the trash. I was forced to conclude it was going to be a two-summer project.

I went ahead and made my way to the cool shade of my favorite tree on the property: the lovers in coitus, my private name for the bald cypress tree and the scrub magnolia tree that had grown out of the cypress tree's trunk during its decades on dry land. The bald cypress tree was over five feet in diameter at the base, over sixty feet tall, thick with needles and Spanish moss. The swamp magnolia was about half as tall as the cypress, with deep green leaves and fragrant small white blossoms. Its limbs spread out wide to embrace the cypress, providing cool shade almost down to the water's edge. I thought there was something quintessentially poetic about the cypress and the magnolia melding together, so different in growth patterns and appearance. I had been indescribably happy when the tree surgeon, who had come out to take down the large, decaying turkey oak, cut up the downed water oak, and appraise the health of the remaining oak trees, had assured me that the magnolia was not endangering the health of the old cypress.

Looking out across the calm lake, I stood, spraying more sunscreen on my arms. Observing the undeveloped waterfront down at the far end of the lake, I thought of my father. In my mind's eye, I saw him taking off his shoes and socks and walking into the water up to his ankles and standing there, taking in the lake. It must have looked primordial, with not a single house on the lakefront. The Martinson's' house, the only house on the lake then, would have been out of his line of sight. I thought his decision to buy his lake property with the money he had saved from his time in the Marine Corps during WWII must have been an emotional purchase, coming as it did in the spring of 1949, three months after my parents had lost their first child, a boy, who had only lived a few days.

My father would have been twenty-nine and my mother twenty, married a little over a year. That event had underlain my otherwise happy childhood. It was never spoken of, but I knew there was something that had happened to make my mother mentally fragile and my father so focused on my mother's well-being. I only found out what it was when I had needed my birth certificate to get my marriage license when I was twenty-three. Seeing on the certificate that a previous child had been born, I immediately understood, like a light bulb had been turned on, the reason my parents lived with an unspoken sorrow. When I asked my mother about the child, she told me he had been born with spina bifida, saying only that it was a long time ago, and she didn't want to talk about it. Emotionally, she shut down, and I knew better than to push the subject any further.

I believed they had bought this lake property as a means to help them heal and come to terms with the baby's birth defect and death. My mother had always loved to fish, and this lake, with its bounty of largemouth bass and brim, was ideal. I had a photograph of her holding a huge bass she had caught, like the ones Lizzy had caught as a girl. This was their place to come and get away from the city and to heal from this tragedy in their young lives.

My dad had carried a heavy emotional burden at that point in his life. He was still dealing with the traumatic effects of the war on his psyche, and he had this tragedy to deal with, too. For some reason, I had always cut my father some slack for his dedication to my mother at the expense of his daughters. I had figured a man could choose to love his wife more than his children, and my father did. I remembered him telling me when he caught me smoking here at the lake when I was a teenager not to let my mother find out. He wasn't concerned that it was a bad thing for me to do, but rather he was concerned about the effect that knowledge would have on my mother. I shook my head. *Parents can't help fucking their children up*, I thought. *They either love them too much or not enough.*

I bent over to pick up my water flask to get a drink. It was decorated with a decal that read "Pretty Is As Pretty Does." The saying was, on one hand, a reminder that where I now lived was the lovely "Deep South" of north central Florida, a place making its way, often kicking and screaming and dragging its feet, into the twenty-first century, already almost one fifth over. Also, it meant to me that good things can happen if you work for them. Looking around me, I knew it would take hard work to clean out this invasive grass to make room for the native water plants, like the graceful purple pickerelweed, but felt that I would do whatever it took to make it so. Smiling to myself, I thought, *Don't get all caught up in imagining this is your fate!* But I did feel there was a fate-like quality to my buying this piece of property. And, I was curious about what fate had in store for me.

Feeling a soft breeze, I thought, *It must be about ten.* Every morning, as regular as clockwork, the wind picked up. Noticing how quiet it was, except for the sound of a lawnmower off in the distance, I headed toward the house to let my two dogs outside. I walked over uneven ground, sunk down in places where trees had once stood. I made a mental note to myself to add sand delivery to my list of things to do.

Walking up onto the tin-roofed back porch, I opened the door, calling to the girls. HB, the English golden retriever, bounded up to be petted, then went out to the yard to find a big stick to content herself with. Hapa, an Australian shepherd mix, took off like the wind, chasing the squirrels and crows down near the waterfront next door, and scaring away the anhinga drying its wings on my neighbor's dock.

Watching them doing the things that made them the happiest, I thought, *We're all so much happier here*. Happiness was an elusive state of being I had chased my whole life. I had finally come to realize it wasn't clearly demarcated. But I felt like moving to the lake had moved me further along the scale toward happiness, realizing, suddenly, that happiness was tied to luck, and I did feel lucky. Thinking this, I picked up my iPhone from the concrete ledge surrounding the porch and typed into the Google search engine, "definition of happy." I stood there, shaking my head when Google pulled up the meaning. It was a Middle English word, which came from the Old Norse word for luck. I had not known that. But, now that I did, it made that elusive state of happiness, while not more concrete, much more understandable.

I also felt fortunate because this area had little in the way of noise pollution to drown out the sounds of the numerous songbirds because the houses on my lake were primarily vacation homes. During the winter I would practically have the lake to myself, while in the summer, it would be busy on the weekends with families enjoying the sun and the water.

I'd learned the lovely couple who owned the quaint, rustic cottage to my left lived in Jacksonville, only coming to the lake occasionally to stay a few days throughout the spring and on the major summer holidays of Memorial Day, July Fourth, and Labor Day. Their huge extended family arrived with them to enjoy it, too. The house to my right was owned by a truly lovely man, Milt, whose mother still lived on the lake. Lizzy had socialized with him and her other friends during her teenage years. This connection with Lizzy made it seem like Milt was more than just a neighbor. Still, he only came by to check his mail after work, preferring to live with his male companion, who lived on the other side of the lake.

Musing about all of this, I called to the girls, and we went in. I gave them a treat for actually coming when I called, petted each of them fondly, and told them how good they were, which was only marginally true, and went back to my room to change clothes. After I had changed into what I thought of as my daily summer uniform of shorts, T-shirt, and flip-flops, I stood at the kitchen counter, eating a late breakfast of peanut butter and jelly on toast and staring at the photographs I had found to put up on my lake bulletin board.

One of the photos was of me at the age of three, sitting in the shallow water of the lake. The background pictured the lake, without a single structure on its shoreline. I stared at the three-year-old me looking up at the photographer, sitting up to my waist in the water, with maiden cane grass and pickerelweed all around me. This lake had always been the place I had felt the most comfortable with myself. Somehow, I had found my way back here like a bird during migration, thinking that this place had been hardwired into my brain from the very beginning of my life.

I put down the photos and looked at the list of things I needed to do, added "get some sand" to the list, and decided to finish unpacking the rest of my moving boxes. I was just tackling a box labeled "kitchen" when my dogs started barking nonstop. Looking through the kitchen window, I saw a bright red golf cart coming up the drive. It was driven by a man who I figured was about my age, straddling that nebulous ground between middle age and old age. I went out to see what he wanted.

He bounded energetically out of his seat.

—Hi neighbor! he said, his southern accent weighing heavily

on his words, I own the property across the street and thought I would come by and introduce myself. My name's Larson McIntyre. Just call me Lars.

—Nice meeting you, Lars, I said, giving him a smile and telling him my name.

He wasn't a tall man, tanned, muscular, and sturdily built, with silver hair and dark-blue eyes. I looked beyond him, through the oak trees, to the other side of the dirt road, seeing his lot with two large, three-sided sheds and a building that resembled a small airplane hangar all standing side by side across the width of the property. I could see a small fishing boat and a pontoon boat in one shed, and in the other was a small RV and a riding lawn mower. The airplane-hangar-looking building was closed. I had never really paid any attention to them before this moment.

He noticed me looking at his property and grinned.

—It's where I store all my toys. I just live about a half a mile from here, over on Lake Hutchinson.

—Looks like the perfect setup to store boats and big things like that, I said, turning to look at him.

—It is, he said, meeting my eyes. Looking back over to his property, he said, Jim Kildare used to own it, the person that owned Milt's place. He asked me if I was interested in buying his house, but I already owned the place on Hutchinson, so I didn't. But, I sort of wish I'd bought it.

—Why is that?

—All my toys would be right across the street . . . and I would be living next to my beautiful new neighbor. He met my eyes. But, he said, I came over to ask you if you would like to come to my house for my pre-Memorial Day celebration this weekend. I do this every year, barbeque ribs and chicken, invite all of my neighbors, my wife's sister and her family, who live over in Starke. Really informal. Don't worry about bringing anything, either.

There'll be plenty. Just come.

—All right, I said, pleasantly surprised. Pre-Memorial Day?

—Yeah, he said, laughing. Through the years I've found that people on the lakes like to have their own Memorial Day parties to kick off the start of the summer. This way, I get to have a big party and everybody comes. Gets them in the mood for their own parties.

—Smart thinking, I said.

—Well, he said, all of a sudden looking serious, you gotta do what you need to do to make things happen.

He hopped back into his golf cart, telling me his address and the time of his party.

—Later, he said as he turned to head back down the driveway. Waving, he honked his horn as he drove away. I watched him speed along in his golf cart down my dirt drive and out onto the clay road. *Beautiful new neighbor?* I may have been new, but I didn't consider myself a beauty. I didn't think I looked any younger than my age, and I hadn't been dressed to impress. But, I figured, maybe flattery was his style of friendliness, and there was certainly no need to take him literally.

---

I pulled my truck up behind one of the many pickups in Lars's yard near the dirt road. As I got out, I could hear the party noise: loud music, with voices in the background. Up ahead I saw smoke and could smell the delicious scent of barbeque. Coming around the side of the house, I saw Lars, gas grill on one side of him and a big industrial-sized smoker on the other. Beyond him, down near the lake, and on his deck, which encircled the house, were about two dozen people or so, their cars and trucks parked on the lawn.

Lars saw me and his face lit up.

—You came!

—Of course, I said, with a smile matching his.

—Up on the deck are cold drinks. Make yourself at home, take in the view of my lake, and introduce yourself to whoever is hanging around up there. I would come, but the meat's almost ready.

—I'll be fine.

I left him, headed for the deck. I had forgotten to ask him which woman was his wife so I could introduce myself, but I figured I would find out soon enough.

Up on the deck, I got myself a Coke and walked over to the railing near a couple who were watching the activity out on the lake. The lake was crowded with motor boats, primarily pulling children on large plastic rafts. One pulled a wakeboarder, while a pontoon boat made laps around the small lake.

—These lakes are sort of like a circus in the summer, aren't they? I said to the couple standing beside me.

The man, with the look of a round-eared elf—short and white-haired with bright green eyes—nodded his head and smiled.

—It's pretty much the same on the lake where I live, he said.

—Which lake do you live on?

—The lake right behind this one.

—That's where I live!

—You do?

I told him my name, and where on the lake I lived. He told me his name, Travis Strickland, introduced his wife, Wendy, and then told me where he lived. We took the conversational path I seemed to follow every time I met someone new who lived on the lake: how long I had been there, how I came to live there, and who else I knew there.

His wife, who had been listening to us talk, spoke up.

—You say your last name is Walker? There was a Jim Walker who used to have a place on the lake.

—My father, I said.

—Wasn't he the old gentleman who rescued you that time the boat motor stopped? she asked her husband.

—Yes! I believe you're right, he said, nodding. Nice man.

I agreed, saying, He sold his place over fifteen years ago, right after my mother died. He bought it before there was anyone else, except the Martinson's, on the lake, back in the forties. It was my family's weekend getaway in the summers. After my sisters and I left home, my mother no longer came anymore, but he made the pilgrimage down here on the weekends throughout the year. He loved it here. I retired from the military and moved back to Jacksonville, but I believe this place was always calling to me, and I'm here to stay.

—We're here to stay, too, Wendy said, smiling at me.

—I was wondering, I said, which of these women is Lars's wife?

Travis and Wendy exchanged a glance. Wendy looked around to see if anyone was near enough to hear her.

—Her name was Shirley.

—Was? I said, surprised.

—She died a little over two years ago from breast cancer. Only fifty-six years old. A lovely person.

—Oh . . . Lars never said anything to me about that, but I guess it's hard working that into a conversation with someone you have just met, I said, as much to myself as to them. When Lars invited me to come to his party—he owns the land across the street from me—he told me his wife's family from Starke would be here. I just assumed she would be here, too.

—He's still coming to terms with her death, said Wendy. She thought he hung the moon, catered to his every whim.

—I can't imagine what that's even like, said Travis, his eyes twinkling as he looked over at his wife.

—No, I don't imagine you can, she deadpanned. He laughed.

I looked from one to the other, amused. Just then, the sound of a bullhorn had us turning in the direction of the amplified voice.

—Everyone! Welcome! said Lars, a big smile spreading across his face. He pointed in the direction of the large pole barn. The food and tables are in my man cave. But before we eat, could everyone bow their heads, and Pastor Bill will say the blessing.

A hefty, middle-aged man, bald-headed with a red face, stepped up to Lars and took the bullhorn,

I watched intently, thinking *Okay* . . .

As a child raised Southern Baptist, going to church had scared the living daylights out of me, what with talk of the damnation of the soul and the promise of spending eternity in the fires of hell if you didn't believe. I had wanted badly to believe since the fires of hell didn't sound like where I wanted to go after I died. And, I knew something of death, since my father's parents had died when I was five, and because they believed, they were always referred to as being with the Lord in heaven.

But as much as I tried, I couldn't believe. I couldn't relate to Jesus or his disciples, especially Paul, who I thought was a holier-than-thou misogynist. As I had gotten older, I had formed the opinion that religion was just a human need to help us try to make sense of our world and a necessary illusion to help tamp down the fear of dying.

As an unbeliever I watched the preacher bow his head.

—Let us pray.

As I looked around me, everyone bowed their heads.

—Heavenly father, thank *you* for this glorious day, for the fellowship of all who have gathered here to enjoy the bounty of *your* glorious feast, for *your* servant Lars and all he does in *your* name. May *your* son, *Jesus Christ*, keep us and bless us, in *your* name we pray. *Amen.*

Lars opened his eyes.

—A*men*, he said, loud enough for all to hear. Everyone! Let's eat!

I turned to Travis and Wendy.

—Do you mind if I sit with ya'll?

—No, of course not! Come on, said Travis. Let's get in line and grab a good seat before they're all gone.

After I had filled my plate with a spoonful each of the wide variety of things people had brought to the party, I moved to sit down, Travis on my left, Wendy on Travis's other side, the seat to my right taken by a young man.

—I don't think we've met, he said as I sat down. My name is Greg Geiger, and this is my wife Tammy, indicating the woman cutting up the food for a toddler sitting in her lap.

—No, I don't think we have, I said, smiling at him and telling him my name.

—Nice meeting you, he said, returning my smile. Do you live on the lake?

—Not this one. What about you?

—No. This is just a summer place. We take turns with the rest of the family using the house next door. He pointed behind him to a red-brick cottage with a chimney. It looked to be about the same age as my father's house.

—That house looks like it has some history, I said.

—It does indeed, he said, grinning. My great-grandfather, a Marine Corps general, Roy Stanley Geiger and his sister owned this house. Now, the extended family shares it in the summer. We don't live far from here, only Orlando, but it seems a world away from our everyday lives when we come here in the summer. I have some really good memories from my boyhood.

—Your great grandfather wouldn't be *the* General Geiger? WWI flying ace and the commander of the First Marine Air Wing, who fought on Guadalcanal during WWII?

—Yes! How do you know who he is? he asked. I've never met anyone outside the family who even knows who he was, much less what he did.

—Heavens! I said. The commander of my father's squadron during WWII had been your great-grandfather's aide-de-camp, and your great-grandfather helped his former aide bring the bomber squadron into being. It was the only Marine Corps squadron equipped to operate at night with radar. The squadron fought on Saipan and Iwo Jima.

—You don't say! Greg said. You seem sort of young for someone whose father fought in WWII.

—Thanks for the compliment, I said, grinning. But, yes, my dad was close to forty years old when I was born.

Travis, Wendy, and Greg's wife had been listening.

—Just think, said Travis. Maybe your dad and General Geiger were down here at their lake places at the same time.

—Like I always seem to be saying, it's such a truly small world, I said, shaking my head, amazed at the connection.

As I got ready to take my leave, I went and found Lars, sitting at a table with two women about my age and, I assumed, their husbands.

I tapped him on the shoulder.

—Lars, thank you so much for inviting me. The food was delicious and your ribs were out of this world.

He looked up at me.

—You're going? I was hoping to get the chance to talk to you a little.

—Well, I don't live far away, and you do have to come over and pick out whichever of your toys you want or need to play with. He smiled. I glanced at the people at his table. They weren't smiling at me, just looking me over. But, I'll see you later. Bye now, I said, as I turned and headed to my truck.

I was working on the grass in the lake when I heard the sound of a golf cart. Lars came racing around the side of my house and down to the waterfront. Getting out of the water to meet him, I raised my hand in greeting.

Hopping out of his golf cart, he smiled, looking at me standing there, wet and somewhat sunburned.

—I just came by to see if you enjoyed yourself, he said, and to hear what you thought of the barbeque.

—It was wonderful! And I enjoyed meeting Travis and Wendy.

—Good! he said. I've probably known Travis the longest of anyone down here. I met him a good ten years ago. He was advertising a pontoon boat for sale, and I went by his house to have a look at it. I didn't end up buying his boat, but we hit it off. When I head up to Michigan to spend the summer with my brother, he always mows my grass and keeps an eye on things for me.

—Sounds like a good friend, I said, reaching down to pick up my towel off the ground and wrapping it around my torso.

—But, he said, I was wondering if you would be interested in having dinner with me this Saturday. I have some amazing salmon that I brought back from Alaska this spring. It would be nice to have someone to share it with, and we could take the opportunity to get to know each other.

—Sure thing, I said, looking at his face more closely.

—I can come over and get you around seven or so.

—Seven works for me, but I can drive myself. I appreciate the offer, really, but you're not even five minutes from me.

—Well, okay, if you're sure. He reached out to touch my shoulder. I nodded my head. Well, I better get home, he said. My sister-in-law and her family are coming over for lunch. We'll spend the day out in the boat, fishing. If I don't see you before, I'll see you on Saturday.

—Roger that, I said, watching him as he got into his golf cart and took off, pedal to the metal.

I decided to go ahead and get dressed and take the girls for a short walk. I got changed into my shorts, T-shirt, and sneakers and put leashes on the girls, and the three of us headed out, down the dirt road in the opposite direction of the paved road. As we walked along, I thought about what Lars had said to me. He had not yet told me his wife was dead and there was no reason for me to think Travis or Wendy had told him that I knew. Did he just assume everyone knew? What did that say about his state of mind? I couldn't help but wonder if Lars's dinner invitation was just a friendly gesture or was it more? Was he lonely? I decided not to get ahead of myself and to just see how things developed. I hoped he was just being neighborly.

I wasn't attracted to Lars physically. He was just a nice man who happened to be my neighbor. I hadn't been attracted to anyone in a very long time. Plus, a romantic relationship with Lars would probably be too much trouble. Complicated as always, it would now be complicated even more by the fact that we both had a lifetime's worth of experiences that had shaped us, not to mention we would both be dealing with the physical aspects of aging in the near future. I thought of this like a game of roulette. Each numbered slot was a particular medical condition under the three large categories of age-related causes of death: cardiovascular disease, cancer, and neurodegenerative diseases like dementia and Alzheimer's, the marble going around and around the wheel until it fell into the slot that would take up all of your time and ultimately end your life. I would have to meet someone exceptional to attempt that game, and the chances of that happening were like winning the Florida Lottery.

As I walked along, I thought of the way human romantic relationships had morphed and changed over my lifetime. Marriage and the difficulty of obtaining a divorce had given way to marriage as a legal tool for combining assets for its positive tax benefits as much as for its traditional role in the raising of children, with the ease of divorce reduced to the undefined phrase of irreconcilable differences. And, with the rise of the LGBTQ+ movement in the last ten years, romance, love, and happily ever after had become more faceted, like a large, radiant diamond. Plus, romance had been affected by the mobile phone's constant presence in the owner's life, in many ways turning a twosome into a kind of foursome. I thought about my sisters' kids, adults now, and the roll of their phones in their dating and romantic relationships, with dependence on dating apps to meet and connect with others of like mind and interests. In this regard, I didn't envy them their youth. Given my introverted nature, if I had been dependent on dating apps to meet someone, with their requirements to share my likes and dislikes and a photo for the world to see, I believe I would have been destined for spinsterhood or, as modern women prefer to call it, being "self-partnered."

On my walk, I started thinking about the three men who had been a part of my life: two of them had been my husbands, and the third man was someone I thought of as the love of my life. I hadn't thought about either of my two husbands in a long time. I had shelved them in a dark closet and had closed the door. Thinking about all three men was like the shuffling of cards, with each of the cards representing my memories—glimpses of how these men gave my life meaning and helped to shape me into the person I had become. There was also the uncomfortable knowledge that I had taken the ease of my existence with my two husbands for granted. Unfortunately, as the saying goes, you don't know what you've got 'til it's gone.

At eighteen, I had met my first husband, Nick, and was struck dumb with his physical beauty. I had gotten a summer job at a shoe store in between my senior year in high school and first year of college. On my first day at work, as the manager was walking me around, we went into the back of the store, where Nick worked stocking the shoes. When the manager called his name, Nick looked up from what he was doing. I looked him in the eyes as we each said hello and "Nice to meet you" to each other. He was the quintessential image of tall, dark, and handsome.

I soon learned he was quiet, intelligent, and an avid surfer, with aspirations to become an architect. He was also kind. We dated exclusively throughout college and had married upon his graduation from architectural school. Our first three years were idyllic: living within throwing distance of Atlantic Beach in a tiny three-room cottage. He worked for a small firm, primarily as a draftsman; I worked at the local bank as a teller; and we spent our free time at the beach. Everything changed when I was accepted to law school. I went to school and he stayed put, and by the time I graduated, our love had been extinguished by our time apart, and we were each living our own lives. In hindsight, I believe that I hadn't been mature enough to comprehend that marriage is more than good sex and doing fun things with someone. It is a serious, long-term undertaking, and a successful marriage takes the trilogy of hard work, compromise, and commitment, not just the elusive idea of love. I left him, feeling empty, believing that there had to be more to life than settling down into an average existence and starting a family. The only thing I had known at the time was that the life I had wasn't the one I wanted.

But my time with Nick had given me a strong belief in myself, a knowledge that I could survive in the world if I just worked hard enough. This came from a combination of my intense law school experience and the fact that Nick and I had no material wealth when we married. But, we were careful, and we were never without a little money to spare. This belief in hard work and not letting life get the best of you have stayed with me. I also learned that, for me, absence did not make the heart grow fonder.

I met Matt at my first law job, as a public defender. Another junior lawyer, he was my age, bright and intense. And, he was adventurous. He didn't think twice about marrying me, quitting his job, and moving with me to Virginia when I decided to join the Marine Corps. And, like me, he didn't want children. Perhaps we had been too much alike. We stayed married for over fifteen years. But, like my marriage with Nick, I had not been committed to it above everything else. The constant moves, my jobs, and our extended times apart took its toll on our relationship until we were just two people living together.

My time with Matt taught me that life was hard. Although sometimes you had periods where the hard part seemed like it was behind you, it was really always there. It also taught me that simplicity in life was not easily achieved when you were living with someone else. There was always a push and pull to long-term relationships, and you either resigned yourself to it and embraced it, or you fought it, making your life an ongoing struggle. Upon my return from Bahrain, I couldn't live like that anymore, and I decided to throw in the towel.

I met Alex, the man I thought of as the love of my life, in my late forties, during my deployment to Bahrain as the US was preparing to wage war on Iraq in 2003. My secret relationship with him was an all-encompassing, self-destructive passion, which burned so hotly, so brightly, and for such a short time. Upon leaving Bahrain, I went through what I can only describe as withdrawal, marked by depression and listlessness. After my divorce, I planned a trip back to the Middle East to see Alex, but didn't go. The rational part of my mind knew that the relationship we'd had was limited to that place and time where we had been stationed together, and there had never been a future for us. I felt this in the hidden places of my soul, too, but after my stroke, I held tightly to my memories of him, using those memories as an impetus to keep going when I felt the world had turned its back on me. He became my personal amulet to ward off depression and help me get out of bed every morning.

But, for the last thirteen years, I had traveled my lone path. And, I seemed committed to that path, simple and unencumbering. I would just have to see tonight what type of relationship Lars had in mind.

---

I had decided to give Lars the impression that I considered this a friendly, two-neighbors-having-a-pleasant-dinner-together event. I wore no perfume or makeup, and I dressed the way I normally dressed: shorts, T-shirt, and sneakers. I got to his house at five minutes till seven, parked my truck up behind his, and walked around to the front of the house, where I found Lars out on his deck. I watched him position a mason jar full of summertime wild flowers exactly in the center of the table.

—I should have asked you if I could bring anything, I said.

—No need. Hope you're hungry.

—I am.

—Well, have a seat. I'll go in and get the food. The salmon won't take long to cook. I didn't want to start cooking it until you got here.

—Nonsense! I said. I'll help you. I'm not comfortable being waited on.

He didn't say anything but led the way into the house. *Gosh!* I thought, taking in the kitchen. It was so clean that even my baby sister, Lizzy, the queen of clean, would have been impressed. The long window that looked out onto the lake and the countertop below it both sparkled in the rays of the setting sun. The wooden countertop looked as if it had been rubbed down with oil, the wood looking beautiful despite all the knife marks cut into its surface. The sink and appliances, all stainless steel, were absolutely spotless. On the counter was a simple green salad with tomatoes and carrots and a loaf of French bread, sliced and toasted, with butter and garlic. Lars went over to the oven to put in the salmon.

—I see what you meant when you said you hoped I was hungry. That is a *huge* piece of salmon! I said, looking over Lars's shoulder as he put the filet, almost as big as the roasting pan, into the upper chamber of his dual oven.

—I love salmon, Lars said, turning on the light of his oven, watching it as it cooked. Salmon is to me what steak is to many people. I like it medium well. He turned to look at me. How do you like it?

—I just eat it however it's cooked. Admittedly, it's usually cooked through. I have never really thought about it.

—I understand that, he said. I'll take it out when it's cooked medium. I'll cut off a piece and finish cooking it for you. You can taste mine to see if you like it my way.

—Sounds good, I said. I'll take the salad and bread out to the table. What are we having to drink?

—What would you like, he said. Beer, water, iced tea?

—Water is great. How about you?

—Water for me, he said. The glasses are right up there, in the cabinet to your right.

I took the food out to the table and then came back to get the water glasses.

—It's a beautiful view of the sunset you have here. From your vantage point, it seems closer than it is from mine. Funny how just a little difference in the angle of the sun creates a different looking sunset.

He turned to look at me.

—This sunlight catches the beauty of your profile.

I raised my eyebrows at him.

—Right . . . Is the salmon ready? He grinned at me.

—Let me take it out. It'll take me just a minute to warm your piece a little more.

—All right, I said. I'm going to go out and enjoy this sunset. Don't be too long or you'll miss it.

Throughout dinner, Lars talked to me about his life: where he was from, his family, what he had done with his life, his wife, how he had met her, and their life together, including the events surrounding her death with cancer. I listened. His words were only a confirmation of my earlier thoughts about his state of mind. His wife's death was all-encompassing for him, and in telling me about his life, he had assumed I just knew that she no longer lived, because that fact sat squarely in the middle of his existence. Rarely did I have to respond, and then only when he looked over at me to see if I was still listening to him. He was on autopilot and, at times, in his own world. When I sneaked a peak at my watch, seeing it was close to nine, I put my hand on his wrist.

—Lars, thank you for the lovely dinner. But, I need to get home to check on the girls.

—You're welcome, he said, looking at his watch. We'll have to do it again, soon.

—Sure. And, I'll cook next time, I said. Don't get up, I'll see my way out. And felt like I had to add, Have a good night, okay?

I got up and walked with purpose to my truck, got in, and breathed a sigh of relief as I turned it around and headed out onto the dirt road, glad I could use the dogs as an excuse to leave, even if they didn't really need to go outside anytime soon. As I drove home, my mind turned on its jukebox.

This was a lasting side effect of my stroke. I had always loved music of all types, and I knew the lyrics to hundreds of songs. Somehow, my rewired brain put money in and often started my mental jukebox playing. This happened all the time, but it was especially noticeable when I wasn't completely awake or when I wasn't focused on a task or when I hadn't slept well or like now, when I was thinking about my dinner with Lars. I had come to think about it like a soundtrack to the movie of my life. My mind decided to play Bob Dylan's classic song, "It Ain't Me, Babe." When my mind had finished singing the song, I wondered how it had come up with the perfect song to capture my situation with Lars. I shook my head, amazed at the complexity and scary workings of the brain.

From everything Lars had told me tonight, it sounded like he was looking for someone as close to his deceased wife as he could find. He wanted so badly to be able to plug into someone who would support him and be there for him the way she had been. He had not asked me one single question about myself. As far as I knew, he was ignorant of anything to do with me, other than the fact that I lived alone on the lake. I had never been a stay-at-home-to-cook-and-clean-and-take-care-of-him kind of person. Never cultivated the nurturing gene. Why he had picked me as a potential substitute for his wife I had no earthly idea. I decided I would invite him over for dinner to reciprocate, and I would have to tell him about myself. I needed to set the record straight.

The next day, Lizzy and her husband, Josh, came down for their weekly visit. The plan was that we were going to put up the magical cypress wood sign, The Walkers', on the oak tree out near the road. When I looked out the window as I heard them pull up in front of the house, I saw they were trailering a pontoon boat. All thoughts of putting up the sign were forgotten as I went out to meet them.

—Well, what do you know? I said, after they had both gotten out of the car, and we stood looking at their pontoon boat.

—I thought it would be nice to have a boat to cruise around the lake in, said Lizzy.

—I wanted something faster, said Josh, looking at his wife, pointedly.

—Our faster days are behind us, said Lizzy, still looking at the boat. She turned to me.

—We sold the Ski Tique we kept over at Daddy's after the kids were grown. Looking at Josh, she said, This is just the speed and size we need. Something big enough for people to sit comfortably with their drink and to lazily cruise around the lake.

—I wonder how fast it will go, he said.

—I guess you can find out after we eat lunch, she said.

After we had eaten the Chinese food they had brought, Josh went back to the guest bedroom to change into his swimming trunks. While Lizzy and I were clearing off the table and cleaning up, I told her about my dinner with Lars.

—You need to nip it in the bud, she said.

—Nip it in the bud?

—It means you need to cut him off from the idea that you're interested in him romantically, right up front, before it goes any further. That is, if that's true.

—It is! I'm not interested in him that way, I said, shaking my head.

—Well, then, you need to save yourself—and him—any confusion by telling him you're not interested in that kind of a relationship with him.

—You're right . . . as always, I said, leaning over to bump her on the shoulder. I do intend to repay his favor by having him over for dinner. I was going to tell him some about myself. Maybe that will scare him.

Josh came up behind us to get down a large plastic tumbler with a lid to fill with ice and water.

—What's she right about this time, and who are you going to scare? he said.

I avoided answering his question.

—What is she never right about?

Lizzy looked over at me, and I smiled.

—Boat ride, Josh? I said.

He looked back and forth between me and his wife.

—Sure. But what were you two talking about?

—None of your business, Lizzy said. Strictly sisters' conversation.

He shook his head and headed out the door.

She watched him through the kitchen window as he got into their car to head down to the lake to put the boat in the water.

—He'd never admit it, Lizzy said, but he often feels at a loss about how to deal with our three-sisters' bond. He's close to his brother, but they don't have the same relationship we do, and it's not really something I can explain to him. I've tried. But, he doesn't understand, so now I just tell him it's none of his business. He always wants to give his opinion—like that's something I want to hear. I set him straight. I told him, "We grew up together in a small house, close in age, all girls. And even though we all took different paths in life; we understand each other's feelings and can relate to them in a way that you have to be a sister in our family to understand. And, well, sweetheart, you're not."

I listened, thinking again that marital partnerships were the most complex and difficult relationships in the world, perhaps because you started out with no foundation and had to build together, mortaring one brick at a time, making sure each was firmly set so the structure didn't come tumbling down. Of course, I hadn't done that, and I realized I was glad I didn't have a marriage partner to deal with anymore. *What did that say about me?* Looking at myself in the best light possible, I decided that I had tried it, and I had never had enough patience, enough flexibility, enough compassion, or enough commitment to last a short run, much less a lifetime. My independence had always been stronger than my love, and I was always too much my own person—too selfish—to sacrifice my own needs or ambitions for those of someone else. I decided I would have to figure out some way to work that into my conversation with Lars when he came over for dinner.

Lizzy and I stood out on Milt's dock waiting for Josh to get back from taking the boat for a spin around the lake.

—Looks like he's enjoying himself, I said.

The pretty blue-and-silver twenty-four-foot pontoon boat seemed to be going as fast as its sixty horsepower engine would push it. Milt and his partner, Conrad, walked down from Milt's house to join us.

Lizzy had told me that Milt was one of those lucky people who had not changed in looks that much since she had known him as a teenager. He had white teeth, dark hair, and a finely-angled face, along with a sunny disposition and sharp wit. Conrad, his partner of five years, was a couple of years older than Milt, with a quiet, easygoing manner. Lizzy told them all about the boat: when and where she and Josh bought it and why they had decided on a pontoon boat.

As Josh brought the boat up to the dock, he was smiling and eager to talk about the boat to Milt and Conrad. The four of them stood there chatting amiably while I listened, thinking how easily Milt and Lizzy had fallen back into a comfortable, almost familial relationship, after almost forty years. They said their good-byes and Milt and Conrad got aboard Milt's small, eccentric pontoon boat, complete with a tin roof, and a life-size metal peacock. We watched them as they took off across the lake toward Milt's mother's place. The American flag at the back of the boat flapped in the breeze as they picked up speed. Then the three of us went aboard the new boat.

—Honey, you should drive this thing! It handles like a dream, Josh said, as he stepped aside for Lizzy to sit down in the captain's seat.

Lizzy squeezed his hand as she sat down to pilot the boat and looked over the controls. I took a seat in the front.

Out on the lake, the sun warmed my face as I took in the shoreline. This north end of the lake had houses on every lot. Many of them still had torpedo grass growing out from the shoreline. As we passed my father's old place, we waved at Tom Wilkinson and his wife, Patsy, out in the water on inner tubes, enjoying the beautiful day.

—I've been meaning to tell ya'll about the alligator Travis saw, I said as we were coming up on his house.

—No! said Lizzy. Who's Travis?

—Yes! I said, smiling at my sister's vehemence, and explained how I had met Travis and his wife.

—I've never seen one on this lake, Lizzy said. Daddy told me that when he bought his place there were a good many alligators back in a boggy corner of the cove. He said they had been—she made air quotes—"disposed of" in the fifties. And, Daddy and his next-door neighbor on the lake Jake Anders caught and killed an eight-foot gator in the early sixties, which came up on their properties during the mating season.

—Well, I said, from what I understood from Travis, it wasn't very big—about three to four feet long. He saw it at dusk. Milt told me that he and Conrad saw it, too, in front of Conrad's place, also at dusk. He said that Conrad reported it to the Fish and Wildlife ranger for this area, who refused to come out and catch it, saying that it had to be at least six feet long before they were authorized to relocate it.

—It must be a budgetary and manpower concern, said Josh. It's understandable from their perspective, but that gator will get big fast, since he has the whole lake for the taking.

—You know, I said, I suspect that baby gator didn't find its way to the lake alone. Probably someone brought it here. The water levels are too low for the natural lake-to-lake migration of gators, especially one so small.

—You just need to keep an eye out when you're in the water, said Josh. But, it's only a matter of time before someone catches it and kills it.

—Well, the sooner the better, Lizzy said.

We cruised close to the shoreline, and Josh got up to stand near Lizzy, both of them keeping a keen lookout for the gator. I sat back, enjoying the beautiful day, thinking.

I hated the idea of killing the small gator, but I also hated the idea of being scared to go in the water or let my dogs go in the water. It was a conundrum I couldn't satisfactorily come to terms with. As we passed along the cypress tree–lined shore, another conundrum I thought about was my father's house being constructed of cypress wood. Growing up I had never thought anything about the building materials that he had used for the house. The smell of the cypress defined it. I had found out the bald cypress tree was protected, and I looked at them in a new light. Every one of them was old and ugly but impossibly beautiful. I couldn't imagine cutting one down and using it for lumber.

But, the most pressing conundrum on my mind this morning was the situation with Lars: his loneliness without his dead wife, compounded by his preoccupation with himself. I understood self-preoccupation only too well, and I recognized it. But, I liked him, or at least what little I knew of him. He struck me as upbeat and intelligent, with a wide range of interests. I would have enjoyed befriending him, not dating him. Like Lizzy said, I needed to figure out how to tell him that soon. And I needed to think about how to tell him while still being neighborly. I didn't know many people here, and the last thing I wanted to do was alienate him. I hoped he wasn't the kind of man who didn't want or know how to be friends with a woman. I had wrestled with this throughout my adult life, a struggle made especially poignant during my twenty years in the Marine Corps, a bastion of heterosexual maleness.

My thoughts were interrupted by the call of "Hi there!" I looked up and saw that we had made it around the cove and Maggie Martinson-Dietrich was standing out on her dock.

The Martinsons at one time had been the only people who lived on the lake and had owned thousands of feet of waterfront property. Maggie and her brothers each had houses, all part of their family compound, but the rest of the land had been sold off by her father thirty years before. Maggie was Lizzy's age, and they had formed a fast friendship when they had met on the lake as young teenagers. Throughout their teenage years, they had been best friends, and their friendship had survived, coming full circle with my move to the lake.

As we neared Maggie's dock, she and Lizzy were already talking across the water about the new boat. Lizzy invited Maggie onboard, and I greeted her, exchanging pleasantries, as she sat down near Lizzy.

As we moved off from the dock, Josh came to sit next to me in the front of the boat, knowing that Maggie and Lizzy would not let him get a word in edgewise.

—How are things with you? I said.

—Good! he said, and he told me about his company's latest potential client and the ongoing competition with other companies that also designed computer software. I listened.

Since we are a communal species, there is nothing surprising about loneliness, but it was a feeling that came to the forefront of my thoughts as I was getting ready the day I was having Lars as my dinner guest.

The previous week, I had kept an eye out for him across the street. When I saw him mowing, I quickly put on my shoes and walked across the street to talk to him. He saw me coming, turned off his big-ass John Deere riding mower, and waited on me, with a big grin on his face. I returned the smile as I walked up.

—What are you doing this weekend?

—Nothing worth mentioning, he said. Why?

—I was wondering if you would like to have dinner with me on Saturday night.

—Sure thing! What time?

—You want to say around six? And, don't worry about bringing anything. I haven't decided what I'm going to fix yet, so it will be a surprise for both of us. I'll let you get back to your mowing.

—Sounds good, sweetie. I'll see you then.

I didn't respond to that, just raised my hand, turned, and walked back to my house. *Sweetie!* I thought. I needed to get this train on the right track, friendly neighbors only. I wanted to make sure his use of the term "sweetie" was just an innocent Southern expression of friendliness, not a term of endearment.

On Saturday, I had decided that I didn't want to wow him with my cooking, not that there was any real chance of that happening anyway. But, I did make some biscuits from scratch to go along with the roast cooked with carrots, onions, and baby potatoes in the crock pot. He arrived exactly on time, and as I led him out onto the back porch, I noticed he was not his usual upbeat self.

—Are you all right? I said.

—Yeah, I'm fine, really, he said, as he sat down at the table I'd set with glasses of water, ceramic alligator salt and pepper shakers, a butter dish, a jar of orange marmalade, steaming biscuits in a basket, and the roast and vegetables in a cast iron pot, with the lid on, to keep them warm.

—This looks great, he said, looking up at me.

—Thanks, I said, sitting down. We'll see.

As I started serving our plates, he launched into another monologue about his wife, this time talking about their bees. That day, he had been in the process of cleaning out the spare bedroom, where he had stored her personal belongings after she died. I figured this activity was the reason he wasn't his usual upbeat self. Among her things were the clothes and some of the paraphernalia she had used to take care of her two bee hives. Telling me that he still took care of the hives, he proceeded to instruct me on the honey bee, their hives, and harvesting the honey. It was fascinating as much for the structure of the complex society of honey bees as for what it took to be their caretaker.

When he came up for air and took a break from talking, I told him that I had some blueberry cobbler.

—As far as I'm concerned, I think dessert should be the first thing eaten and not the last, I said.

—I'm not much of a sweet eater, he said, but I'll have a small piece.

—Ice cream or whipped cream on top?

—No, thanks, he said, smiling. I'm only having some because you made it for me.

I didn't respond to his last statement. Figuratively biting my tongue, I went into the house to get the cobbler. I cut two pieces and put ice cream on mine, thinking, *Lars and I live on different planets*. I brought out the pieces of cobbler and sat back down.

—Next week, I'm leaving to go up to spend the summer with my brother and his family in Michigan, Lars said.

—I remember you mentioned going there, when we talked about Travis mowing your yard while you were gone. He nodded.

—My brother's a good shit—pardon my French. I don't like to cuss in front of ladies. It's an expression meaning he's a super guy.

I just nodded my head. I certainly knew what the term meant, and I didn't consider myself a lady, which had derogative connotations for me of someone who needed to be protected and didn't need to be involved in decisions. *Don't get aggravated*, I told myself.

As I ate my dessert, he told me all about helping his brother this summer with his cherry orchard and all the things that went along with picking the cherries, a crop that was highly perishable, and getting them to market. I listened, resigned that I wasn't going to have the opportunity to tell him anything about myself.

He was just getting warmed up to his subject when Hapa started barking from the back bedroom.

—Sorry, I said. Sounds like I need to take her outside for a walk before it gets dark.

The sky had started to darken, the sun covered by dark clouds, like it might rain. I got up from the table, and he rose as well.

—Dinner was great. We'll have to take it from here when I get back.

—When are you leaving? I said.

—Monday morning, bright and early. He stood there looking at me. If I were a betting person, I would have bet a hefty sum that he was preparing to kiss me goodnight, to set the scene for when he returned.

—Have a good trip and drive safe, I said, moving back a step. I better go back and get her before she has an accident. If you don't mind, you can see yourself out. You don't need to go back through the house.

He looked at the closed door to the house, looked off the porch into the yard, then he looked at me. I smiled, raised my hand in good-bye, and went into the house. When I came back out, he was gone.

As I cleared off the table and washed the dishes, I thought again about Lars's preoccupation with himself. It embarrassed me that I had always been so preoccupied with myself. Maybe that's one of the reasons Lars missed his wife so much: there was no one to adore him now. He needed the attention and was lost without it. Also, I thought that the dream of being in a relationship was very different than the reality. The reality seemed like a heavy burden. A bundle filled with that person's wants, needs, and desires. I realized that I had never been realistic about the role of a partner in my life, always setting myself up to be disappointed in them. I wasn't sure why, deciding the answer was something that was buried deep in my psyche. I comforted myself with the knowledge that I at least recognized that tendency now. It wasn't much of a comfort, but it was something I had never admitted to myself before, and like other things I had admitted to myself since my stroke, it made me feel like I knew myself better.

I'd have to tell Lizzy that I didn't get a chance to "nip it in the bud." Lars would be gone all summer, and maybe he would come back from Michigan less focused on himself. Maybe I could figure out a way to maintain a neighborly relationship with him. Stranger things had happened, and I could only hope.

# Isn't She Lovely

In early August, I woke up to a light rainfall, the remnants of the downpour that had blown through the area during the night. When I took a look at my rain gauge, I saw that I had gotten almost three inches of rain. Thunder storms and the accompanying hard rain had always been a part of the North Florida summer weather pattern when I had been a girl. I didn't know if it was the warming planet, better forecasting models, the entertainment quality of the weather forecasts, or a combination of the three, but from late July through late September, weather reporting took on the role of foreboding fortune-telling, from forecasts of dangerous lightning storms, golf ball–sized hail, and flooding rains to the real boogie man, the deadly hurricane. The previous days forecast of high winds, flooding, lightning, and potential tornados was the first of the season, and I was worried the weather was going to dampen, literally, the highly anticipated sister's weekend.

This was a yearly weekend event, which had evolved after Helen's death. When she died, I was still in the Marine Corps, having just returned to Jacksonville, and still looking for a house to buy. The surprise to find she had made me the sole beneficiary of her estate, my immediate insistence that my other two sisters share equally, the resulting hassle of sorting out the mess of her monetary affairs, and the selling of her house and my parents' home, which she had inherited from my father, brought the three of us together in a shared purpose, perhaps in a way no other event could have done. As a way to commemorate the sale of my parents' house, we took a weekend trip to a Florida state park, renting one of the cottages. We cooked our meals together and spent the weekend just talking and reminiscing about our girlhoods. We all enjoyed the weekend so much, we decided to get away together for a weekend every year.

Normally, it was planned around going somewhere within driving distance, although one year we had gone as far away as Virginia's outer banks to see my father's last surviving sibling, his only brother, Bill. This year we had chosen this particular weekend because Bill's two daughters, Sybil and Angie, were coming to visit. All of us had been close as children and had spent summer vacations together at the lake. They were excited to visit the lake again after all these years, and it seemed perfect to combine their visit with our annual get-together.

I bought matching T-shirts for all five of us that read "Keep it Simple," one of my favorite expressions from my days in the Marine Corps, where it was called the KISS principle, "Keep it Simple, Stupid." The intention was to wear them everywhere we went over the course of the weekend, an outward sign of our solidarity during our time together. And, we would cook together, another form of bonding and something our mother insisted upon when we all lived at home. Sybil and Angie were on board with that, too. I had told them that this was the one time of the year we could be together, at a point in our lives where we could appreciate each other and our shared experiences of girlhood.

And, like always, one of the activities would be a tournament featuring the board game Aggravation. As children, we had all liked the game so much that our Uncle Emery had made two wooden playing boards, one for us and one for Sybil and Angie. He also supplied the different colored marbles for the game. We had discovered our board and the marbles, which were still housed in a glass peanut butter jar, when we had gone through our parents' belongings after my father's death back in 2004. We had immediately stopped what we were doing and played the game until one of us had eventually won three games. Even then, when Helen was still alive, it was something the four of us could do together. At least for that short period, we put aside our differences and any issues we had with each other to just revel in the pure joy of the game. This year we would be playing on the six-players side of the board, another thing we had not done since we were children when Sybil and Angie played with us. I couldn't recall if they loved the game as much as we did, but I suspected the game held a special place in their memories as well.

---

Later that morning, the sun shining brightly and not a cloud in the sky, Cora and Lizzy arrived in Lizzy's car, a pristine silver Lexus SUV. Having seen the car coming up the drive, I went out to meet them, smiling and wondering what they had talked about during the hour drive to my place.

Cora got out of the car first, moving like a five-foot-tall version of the roadrunner from the old cartoons, slamming the door, quickly moving to the back of the car, waiting on Lizzy to open it so that she could get out her overnight bag. Her thick, light-red hair, looking recently cut and expertly styled, swayed in sync with her quick movements. She was dressed very sensibly in a simple white blouse, navy trousers, and white tennis shoes. Simplicity and sensibility characterized Cora's life. She had known exactly what she wanted from life since the summer she was sixteen years old. Working as a candy striper at the children's wing of Baptist Hospital, she saw children ravaged by life-threatening illnesses. That experience sealed her fate. She wanted to be a doctor. And, she wanted to be married; to have two children, a girl and a boy; and to live happily ever after. She had achieved everything except the happily ever after part.

Cora had become a pediatrician, and she had met her husband, Carson, and married him at medical school. But somewhere along the way, her husband figured out he preferred the sexual company of men and he left Cora. This had all happened while I was still in the Marine Corps, so I didn't experience the tragedy this was for her firsthand. But, it was something she couldn't fix. She shared with me that Carson had told her he was going to move in with his friend Michael so he could have a chance to think, and they could go through marriage counseling, only to find out later that Michael was his lover. It had been over ten years since her divorce, and she seemed to have recovered her vitality, focusing her substantial intellect and energy on her daughter's two young children.

Lizzy moved at a more leisurely pace. Her silver, shoulder-length hair coordinated perfectly with her floral-patterned, pale-blue blouse, white linen pedal pushers, and sandals. It was unusual to see Lizzy without Josh, her husband of thirty-two years. They had the kind of marriage people often dream about: best friends and life partners, with a relationship that sparkles with laughter and good-natured banter. They had two children, and their oldest, Samantha or Sammy, was expecting her first child later this year. Lizzy and Josh were both beside themselves with joy over the upcoming event.

As soon as the back hatch of Lizzy's car began opening, Cora reached in and grabbed her suitcase. I moved to the back of the car to help with the bags.

—Hi Julie! she said, giving me a big smile as she headed toward the house.

In the back of the car, I saw a huge ice chest, four bags of groceries, five new beach chairs, and Lizzy's overnight bag.

—Guess we're the ones designated to unload the car, she said, grinning. I grinned back at her.

—Good drive down?

Lizzy gave me an amused smile and shake of the head.

—Fine. I arched my eyebrows at her, and she said, It's nothing, really. You'll see.

I reached for the ice chest, and followed her into the house, anticipating the unfolding of this small mystery. Cora was fond of secrets, and I figured she must have told Lizzy one of them on their way to the lake. After we brought in the bags of groceries, Lizzy took her things back to "her" room, the guest room. After I bought the house, I had told her, "This room is yours. And, this house will be yours when I die. This lake is as much a part of your life as it is mine, maybe more."

She reached over and hugged me, long and tight, saying, —You're sure?"

—Yep, I said. —I don't believe I've ever been surer of anything in my life."

Cora came out of my bedroom, where I had told her she and I would sleep. Sybil had told me she and Angie wouldn't mind sleeping on my pullout couch in the study.

—I'll start putting the refrigerated things away, Cora said.

—Okay, I said, as I started unpacking the groceries and organizing the ingredients into the meals we would cook over the weekend.

Lizzy soon joined us.

—I'll set the table for lunch, she said. Cora, leave out the sandwiches I picked up at Lola's.

Sandwiches in front of us and the ice tea poured, we sat down for lunch.

—On the drive down, Cora said, Lizzy and I talked about the three of us going out to Miriam and Emery's farmhouse on the way to the airport in Gainesville. I want to take a better picture of it than is in the book Rachel has on cracker houses . . . to give to my architect.

—Your architect? I said, surprised.

I looked over at Lizzy. She gave me a barely imperceptible nod, saying nothing, simply drinking her ice tea.

—Yes, said Cora, looking first at me, then at Lizzy. I was telling Lizzy on the way down that Rachel and I hired an architect in Gainesville. Someone who specializes in cracker houses. We have been talking about getting started on a house on the land I bought in Grandin.

—That's great news! I said, surprised at this new wrinkle in Cora's life. The land that they sold in the sixties is a subdivision now. It should be pretty easy to find.

—I don't remember the farm, said Lizzy. I was only four years old when they sold it. But, I'm curious to see it. Let's kick off this sisters' weekend by finding it.

We made the turn off of State Road 26 onto County Road 1469, a narrow, two-lane road with oak woods and pine scrub brush on both sides. Our car was the only one on the road.

—Let's look and see if the big live oaks that used to hang over the road are still here, I said. I remember the turn off to their drive was right after those trees.

As we came around a sharp turn, I saw them.

—Those are the trees. I pointed ahead at the huge live oaks, which looked the same as I remembered from fifty years earlier. Beyond them on the right, we saw a subdivision sign, with the words "Blueberry Landing," surrounded by small ornamental plants.

—Blueberry Landing? said Lizzy.

—This has got to be the place, I said. I understand why they gave it that name. Wasn't that place Daddy went to buy his blueberry plants around here somewhere?

—You're right, it was! said Cora.

—Yes, it *was*, said Lizzy, grimacing. I spent hours and hours there with Daddy.

I smiled, remembering all the different desserts, jams, and jellies my mother had made from the blueberries my father had grown. Lizzy had gotten the brunt of my father's blueberry-growing passion.

—We're lucky it's not a gated community, said Lizzy, making the turn into the subdivision.

The houses were large, set back from the road, and landscaped lavishly with azaleas, lily of the valley, dogwoods, and other plants perfectly suited to the climate. We followed the twisting road, stopping when we came to a tee intersection. Lizzy looked both ways.

—Any idea which way?

Up ahead I could make out Little Lake Santa Fe through the trees. The crossroad ran parallel to the lake. Farther down to the left, the road turned toward the water.

—Let's go left. If it's not there, we can always backtrack.

Lizzy nodded and was just getting ready to turn left when a six-foot-long rattlesnake appeared, slithering so quickly that, if we hadn't been looking where it had crossed the road, we would have missed it. We sat there watching it disappear quickly into the grass by some azaleas. I looked at Lizzy.

—It's gone now.

—I hate snakes! she said, with an emotion she rarely exhibited, watching intently the place where we had last seen the snake.

Cora leaned forward in her seat.

—What kind of snake?

I turned to look at her.

—A diamondback, I said in a stage whisper.

—I don't know why rattlesnakes scare me, said Lizzy. I've never been bitten or even had a close call with one. It's irrational, I know.

—Everybody has something they're irrational about, I said. I'm that way about small spaces. What about you, Cora?

—Nothing, she said quickly. There is nothing I'm irrational about.

—Okay, I said, turning my head to look at Lizzy as she turned left. The look on her face broadcast what she was thinking. It was what that same look had always said, ever since she had been a little girl: *Oh, give me a frigging break!*

Up ahead, the road made a sharp curve and veered right. At the end of the road was a huge magnolia tree in full bloom. Its limbs curved down to the ground on all sides, like I had only seen with ancient live oaks. Its white blossoms seemed to radiate light. As we got closer, I saw the farmhouse, tucked behind the big tree.

—It looks so much smaller than I remember, I said, shocked at the fact it was not a huge mansion, just a large cracker-style house.

Lizzy pulled off the narrow road and we all got out. There was no one out in the yard, and I didn't see a car anywhere. The small front yard of thick green grass was surrounded by small shrubs and flowering plants. It was enclosed by a low stone wall, which ran along the road and disappeared into the trees near the lake. Off to the right of the farmhouse, far enough away so that you could barely see it, there was another large house.

Cora, walking ahead of Lizzy and me, positioned herself in front of the house, setting her elbows on the wall as she took a few pictures with her phone.

—You're right, Julie, about the house looking so small, she

said. You hear people say that all the time when they see something again that they hadn't seen since they were children. But I've never experienced it before now.

—I don't see the cattle gap, either, I said.

Cora looked around behind me, gauging where she remembered it being.

—They must have had to take it out when they paved the road.

—I bet you're right, I said.

—I wish I could remember, but, I just don't, said Lizzy. It just looks like an old cracker house to me, not some magical, enchanted place like it is for the two of you.

The building was a classic cracker house, an example of Florida's wood-frame vernacular architecture. Built in the mid-1800s of first-growth oak and pine, it was a four-room Georgian-style house with a hallway running through the middle and a kitchen down another long hallway off to the right side, with ceilings over ten feet high. Tin-roofed with a cupola, its roof extended over the porches on the front and the rear of the house. I remembered it had been painted white, with the paint peeling in places, and the front steps were red brick, made by my father to replace the original wooden steps. It looked to have been restored to its original grandeur. The outside was freshly painted a light gray. The tin roof and the windows looked to have been replaced, as did the sagging roof of the porte cochere on the left side of the house. I was glad to see the old girl was being taken care of.

When Cora finished taking her pictures, we got back in the car and headed back the way we had come.

—Let's go straight and have a quick look at this area while we're here, I said when we got back to the tee intersection. If these houses are any indication, it must be a really pretty neighborhood back there along the lake.

—What time does their plane land? said Lizzy.

—Not till almost four o'clock, I said, checking the e-mail Sybil had sent me with their flight information.

—All right, said Lizzy. Cora?

—Sure thing. I don't remember ever being back here before.

—Well you wouldn't, I said, turning around to look at her. There were no roads here. This was part of the pecan orchard. See?

To our right and left, as we drove along the narrow road which curved left toward the lake, were the remains of an orchard. The pecan trees, covered in Spanish moss, were sparse, but if I closed my eyes, I could see the long rows and columns of trees in both directions.

As we got closer to the lake, I could see that the buildings down here were not part of the subdivision we had just come from. Many of them were small houses, apparently built before the subdivision, and the remainder of the residences were double-wide trailers. The lots were narrow, many separated by chain link fences, and each property had a shed covering a water well and pump. There were different-sized boats, mostly small fishing skiffs, some sitting on boat trailers out in the open and others under makeshift sheds. One property even had what looked like a war memorial, a small concrete area with a tall flagpole flying the American flag on top and the POW flag below it.

—Was this part of Miriam and Emery's property? asked Lizzy.

—I can't imagine it was. It's definitely not part of the subdivision. Seeing these trailers and the junky yards makes me feel like such a snob.

—Snob? said Cora, leaning forward in her seat.

—Yep. I know that a lot of good people can't afford to build a house on a lake these days, but you would think if you were lucky enough to live here, you would want to keep it as nice as possible, just to reflect the beauty of the lake, if for no other reason.

—Jules, said Lizzy, I'm thinking that these people are sitting on a gold mine. Someday soon these small homes and trailers will be replaced by houses bigger than the ones we passed back there. You won't be able to get back here because this community *will* be gated. Would that make you happy?

—Jules? said Cora, before I could respond to Lizzy. Where did that name come from?

—It's what Colonel Wallace, the officer in charge of all the law centers on Okinawa, called me. My nickname. Everybody in the Marine Corps called me Jules. Except Matt, he called me Nadine.

She nodded.

—Jules. I like it.

They both smiled, and Lizzy turned the car around, making her way back to the tee intersection.

—Nadine, Cora said, as she moved up on her seat, with her head poked between us. Where did he get that name from?

—It's a name from a movie we saw. The actor who plays the husband of the character Nadine says, "When you're right, you're right, and even when you're wrong, you're right."

—Interesting, said Cora, nodding her head. Sounds like something people could say about all three of us. She grinned at me. Lizzy looked over at me, saying nothing, but she was grinning, too.

—You know, I said, maybe I feel so snobbish about not having junky houses on this lake because it was a part of my life that was inordinately special. Miriam and Emery's farmhouse on beautiful Little Lake Santa Fe was a magical place. Somehow I can't get over the idea that I lost something when they sold it. But I'm not really sure what that something is.

—It's ancient history now, over fifty years ago, Lizzy said, amused. I wouldn't worry about it.

—You're right . . . of course! I said, looking at Lizzy.

—Me, too, Cora said.

—Me, too, what? said Lizzy

—I felt like I lost something, too. But, like Julie—I mean Jules—she said, smiling, I'm not really sure what to call it. Maybe that's why I'm thinking about building a house on Lake George that was like the one Miriam lived in. Rachel loves cracker houses and it would remind me of Miriam.

—What about Emery, Lizzy said.

—What about him? Cora said. I never liked him.

—I didn't *not* like him, I said, but to little girls, he was an intimidating person, and he *did* make the Aggravation board for us.

—He was a drunk, said Cora, her tone indicating that the conversation was over.

I knew that Cora had always idolized Miriam, our father's favorite sister. Miriam had been quiet, kind, and strong in character, and the fact that Cora's face resembled Miriam's helped in that heroine worship. I decided I would just quit the discussion before it turned into an argument, one I didn't have a particular passion for. So I said,

—He was.

---

We arrived at the airport about a half an hour before our cousins' flight was scheduled to land. The flight from Charlottesville was a direct flight and was right on time. When the announcement was made that the flight had arrived, we all craned our necks, looking expectantly at the passengers as they began flowing through the arrival gate. We had no trouble spotting them. They looked just like older versions of the girls I remembered: freckled, slim, tall, and blond.

A year younger than me, Sybil had been athletic as a girl. An outdoorswoman, she and her family had spent their vacations hiking and camping all over the US, Europe, and Australia. Her husband was also athletic, as were her two adult children.

Angie, two years younger than Sybil, looked more like Sybil's twin than just her sister. But unlike her sister, she was a widow, her husband having died from lung cancer two years earlier.

—Cousins! Over here! Cora called out as we all three waved.

There were hugs and air kisses all around, with much squealing of pleasure, and then on the drive home, excited talk, exchanging years of news—what everybody was doing now, with a primary focus on what everyone's children were up to these days. Then, talk turned to the lake.

—You know, I said, all things considered, it hasn't really changed at its core. What I mean is that the lake—its fresh, clear water, its wildlife, and just the feel of Melrose—hasn't changed. Of course, it looks different now, with houses all along its waterfront, and the water level of the lake has gone down substantially since we were kids.

—It's not just our lake, said Lizzy. The big lakes, Geneva and Brooklyn, are very shallow and are just pale reflections of their former selves.

Cora put in her two cents.

—Even south of Keystone, at my lot on Lake George, the water has gone down, too. And, it's not a spring-fed lake. It's tied into the streams and waterways of the state.

—But not to worry! I said, seeing Angie's and Sybil's faces take on a look of concern. The lake is still beautiful. It's just changed with the times, like we all have.

—Isn't that the truth, said Angie, shaking her head. I recently started going to the gym to work out on the weights and ride the exercise bike. Understand, this is something I did religiously when I worked. But, heavens! I didn't remember it being so hard. Both my sons tell me to take it easy because I'm old! I told them both "I . . . am . . . not . . . old! I'm just aging, like a fine wine." They both laughed at me.

—I've made peace with the whole aging process, Sybil said. I'm not saying that I'm okay with it or that I'm happy to be getting older, but it's just easier to accept it since there is nothing I can do about it. After I retired, if I hadn't been taking care of Mother, I'm not sure what I would have done with my time. And since she died six months ago, I've been working on getting her affairs in order. When I'm finished wrapping that up, I'm going to have to figure out what to do with myself.

—I'm lucky, said Cora. I volunteer some at the Saint Lucia Center. To Sybil and Angie she said, It's an endowment center for child care. A place where people who can't afford a pediatrician can bring their children for care. And, I pick up my two grandchildren from school and keep them in the afternoon until Rachel and Roger get home from work. She looked around at everyone packed into Lizzy's SUV. I'll have to tell you about them this weekend. Lizzy and Julie—I mean Jules—are probably sick of hearing about them, but they love them, too.

—Jules? said Sybil. I again explained where my nickname had come from.

—I like it, said Angie. Aren't you glad it's not a nickname that would make you cringe? Jules is nice.

—Thanks, I said, nodding, and turned around in my seat to smile at her.

—Maybe it's just me, Lizzy said, but I think it's going to be easier for me than it's going to be for Josh. I'm dreading the day he retires. Already, we sort of drive each other crazy since we both work from home.

—Do you? said Sybil. What's that like? Working from home, I mean, not driving each other crazy!

We all laughed.

—Well, Josh has been working from home for over ten years. Since he works in IT, he was ahead of the curve with the whole working from home movement. I only work part time for the Episcopal church, and since I work on keeping up the website, I get more work done in a shorter period of time by working from home than I would if I went into the office. We are together so much that sometimes I think we need to take separate vacations just to have some time apart.

Everybody looked at her and she noticed.

—I'm lucky, really. In all things. But there *can* be too much of a good thing, you know?

---

After sunset, we all took one of the new beach chairs and headed down to the lake to sit around the Tiki smokeless fire pit. It was a beautiful night, with a light wind out of the east and a clear night sky. We didn't need a fire for warmth, but it created a cozy glow, the perfect ambiance to talk about what was dearest to the hearts of my two sisters and cousins—their children and grandchildren.

I listened, well, I half-listened. I knew better than to say anything that could be construed as critical. My sisters were blinded by their love of their children and there was no reason for me to think that my cousins didn't feel the same way about theirs. I figured it would be much the same with their grandchildren. I tried to evince interest in the conversation about my cousins' grandbabies by asking how old they were when they started walking or talking, and I smiled in wonder when there was talk about their grandbabies' budding intelligence, enchanting personalities, and the adorably horrible things they had done, like drinking from the toilet. I looked at photos of the kids, trying to act enthralled, as my cousins passed around their phones and described what the different pictures portrayed—for them, the most wonderful of scenes. But part of my mind was thinking about the broader issue of procreation and how it was at the center of everything we did in this amazing world.

Cora's first pregnancy ended in miscarriage, and I remember how devastated she had been afterward, going through what I can only describe as a period of clinical depression. I comforted her the best I could, but although I believe I was compassionate and sympathetic, I couldn't be empathetic. Six months later, she became pregnant, and all her feelings of depression over the lost fetus dissipated. When Rachel was born, it was as if nothing could ever produce the feelings of success, pleasure, or accomplishment that having that baby gave Cora.

I remember being perplexed about these postpartum feelings of hers. She was scarily intelligent, and I knew she would have been considered mentally gifted in today's way of thinking. She graduated from high school at sixteen, with straight A's in the most advanced courses that were offered at that time. Then, she completed undergraduate school with a major in chemistry and a minor in psychology at nineteen. She graduated from medical school at twenty-two and finished her residency requirements by her twenty-fifth birthday. At the time of Rachael's birth, Carson appeared to be a loving and caring husband. However, those facts paled in comparison to motherhood.

I had come to the simple realization that the main purpose of living is to procreate. I thought it made perfect sense that the body makes sex such a pleasurable and sensual experience for itself. The body is so focused on the goal of giving life, that its pheromones work like a love potion, bringing disparate people together, making their offspring's genes more diverse in order to evolve. And when you throw in the love hormone, oxytocin, created by the body in excess during sex and even more in pregnancy, you have the secret ingredient for close emotional bonds. I knew there was much more to the process than that, but I saw the body as an organism supremely engineered to procreate.

Cora and I had grown up in the era when it was becoming common for women to abandon full-time childcare in order to pursue a career. But, women had never abandoned the idea of having babies. Most women wanted to do both. Cora was a perfect example of the term "super mom." After Rachel's birth, she put her career on hold and had her second child, Benjamin, less than two years after Rachel. Her dream accomplished, a girl and a boy, she resumed her career as a pediatrician, working on staff at the Hope Haven Children's Hospital and balancing that with all the things she didn't want her children to miss out on: music lessons for Rachel; sports for Benjamin, like baseball and soccer with all the home and away games; birthday parties; involvement in their local Episcopal church; and a myriad of other activities like summer vacations at different national parks and summer camp, where she volunteered as the on-staff doctor while her kids were there. With her intelligence and energy, if she had been a man, she could have made the decision to do breakthrough medical research or to even just pursue a full-time medical career. But as a woman, her driving instinct had been to tend to her children first, her husband second, and her career third.

I always thought about human population growth when I read about havoc caused by fire, flooding, drought, or the destruction of forests and other habitats that directly impact the extinction of different species. I knew our population growth wasn't just caused by childbirth in the US, since America prided itself on immigration, but I did believe our country, and the world, were overpopulated. I had read a newspaper article with a picture about the heat wave that was hitting the interior of China. The picture was of people, with plastic inner tubes around their bodies, seeking relief in the water of a man-made lake. All of the people were smiling at the camera. But what struck me was that the photograph, from edge to edge, showed dozens and dozens of people packed tightly together in the water. The idea of sardines packed into a can of oil came to mind. It actually made me shudder in horror.

I had always prided myself on turning my back on my body's calling to procreate. I felt that I had been born at the right time in history, when birth control pills were easy to obtain. For me, the chance of getting ovarian cancer somewhere off in the distant future was a small, inconsequential risk compared to the freedom from pregnancy and a semblance of control over my future afforded by that little pill. Also, I arrogantly thought of myself as above the common fray of people who were primarily focused on having children. After all, I had become a lawyer, making the decision not to have children so I could pursue my career. At least, that was my reason . . . or excuse.

In listening to my sisters and cousins talk, I admitted to myself that the simple fact of the matter was that pregnancy and having a child had scared the daylights out of me. I was afraid of having a child born with a terrible birth defect who would die, like my mother's first child. It had been this simple and unadulterated fear which had kept me from having a child, not concern about overpopulation. I also thought there was a deeper fear: the fear of losing myself by loving too much.

My mother had loved me too much. My birth, seven years after she had lost her first child, was an event that brought her back to the land of the living. It had secured her place in the world as the mother of a healthy child, one that she doted upon. I had always felt loved, something that I took for granted growing up, but I also felt trapped, not quite suffocated but more like a caged bird. It was only when I left Jacksonville for the Marine Corps that I felt like I had flown the coop.

Looking over at Lizzie, fully engaged in the conversation going on around me, I thought about what she had said about she and Josh working from home: that there can be too much of a good thing. I thought that my mother loving me so much had been too much of a good thing. It was a smothering love, not one she thought I needed but rather something she had needed to do for herself.

In my family's story, my mother wasn't a person whom my sisters ever talked about. She had been the mighty queen bee. As children, we were like moons orbiting around her. She always had the final word about anything we were allowed to do; she was the one who dispensed the money for us to use. And she was the undisputed center of our father's world. She had been someone whom it was impossible for us girls to get close to: secretive, authoritative, and self-centered. I had not only been afraid of having children, but I didn't want to turn out to be a mother like my own. As it turned out, I had only managed not to be secretive or authoritative.

This line of thinking brought me back around to my childlessness. It's fair to say I wasn't as concerned as my sisters or cousins with global warming or the need to figure out how to move from fossil fuel to some other more environmentally friendly form of energy. They felt like they had a stake in the future viability of the planet, while I did not. But, in looking around at them, their faces glowing in the light from the smoldering embers, I told myself I should try to be as hopeful for their children and grandchildren as they were. I should be happy for their joy in having had physically perfect children, who survived to have their own physically perfect children, children who could hopefully contribute something to society, perhaps even achieve great things. I secretly hoped they would do more with their lives than just having their own children. But it was not for me to judge.

As I sat there listening to them talk, I reveled in the fact that returning to the lake had created a tighter bond with my sisters. My mental jukebox decided to play Stevie Wonder's, "Isn't She Lovely." This song had never been a favorite of mine, for obvious reasons, but I couldn't argue with my mind when it decided to play a song.

# Late for the Sky

Out of the blue of the western sky! I had always loved that expression for things that were totally unexpected and not in a bad way. That's the way I felt in early September when I received the e-mail from Nick, my first husband, suggesting that we have lunch together. He wrote that he had heard from his sister Martha that I had moved to the lake, and he was excited for me. He thought it seemed appropriate that I had ended up there. He had visited the lake with me many times, primarily when we were both attending college nearby, and now that I thought about it, he, more than any other person except my sisters, knew what the lake meant to me.

I had seen Nick several times over the years since I had left Jacksonville for the Marine Corps. The first time was when I returned home to visit my parents during my PCS move from Japan to Washington, DC. Matt had not come with me, since he was already attending Amphibious Warfare School in Virginia, making it easier for me to just focus on my family visit. I had found out from my mother that Nick's mother was dying, and I went by her house to see her. Nick's mom had been like a second mother to me, and we visited, just the two of us, back in her bedroom. I didn't stay long, and it was more like she was comforting me than I her as she held my hand and talked to me about everything and nothing.

While I was with her, we heard Nick and his wife come in, their voices soft, talking with his sisters who were there. I hurriedly made my good-byes, going out the back door, with the intention of avoiding having to talk to Nick. But, he intercepted me as I was getting into my father's car. He wanted to introduce me to his wife. I looked at him with "Why?" written all over my face. He smiled at me.

—She won't bite. At least I don't think she will. She wants to meet you.

I followed him back into the house, walking through the kitchen, warm and inviting, with the feel of constant use. The memories of all the time I had spent in that house made me sad because the lovely and safe life this house represented hadn't been the one I wanted. I had buried those memories, and all I wanted to do was to get the hell out of there before they all bubbled further to the surface.

His wife, Marjorie, or Marge, as Nick called her, was sitting on the living room couch breastfeeding their son. Eight years younger than me, she was long-legged, busty, blonde, and blue-eyed, with a triangular-shaped face and dimples. Physically, she was everything I was not. Nick introduced us.

—He's hungry, I said, inanely.

She was looking me over, not smiling, and she said,

—He is.

I caught the look in her eyes that was universal when the current love is meeting a former love: what did he see in you? I wasn't immune from those sorts of thoughts either. My first impression of her was that she was bourgeois. That word had a negative connotation to me, implying that she was not in the least extraordinary but just a physically attractive woman who wore expensive clothes, pale nail polish, and too much makeup. I decided she was only breastfeeding because it was the trendy thing to do and not because it was what was best for the baby. I had no evidence of this, and my thoughts were completely irrational. I made the snap decision not to like her, and I believe she did the same thing.

I got out of there as quick as I could, making the lame excuse that my mother was expecting my sisters and their families over for dinner and she needed my help. Nick walked me back out to my car.

—I'm glad you came by to see Mother, he said.

—Me, too.

*I'm sorry for the heartache caused by our divorce, and I hope you are happy with your life* was right there, unsaid between us, as he closed my car door and waved good-bye.

Eight years later, I returned alone to Jacksonville to attend my mother's funeral. Nick came to her funeral with two of his sisters, and afterward, he alone went to the post-funeral gathering at Cora's house. He and I sat on her terrace, which backs up to open woodlands in south Jacksonville, near the river. It was April, and the woods were filled with budding dogwoods and redbuds, and everything was so green. We talked about our lives. I told him about working for the Secretary of the Navy, the places we had visited, and what it had been like living in Hawaii. He told me about his work and his growing family, three small children, all boys. At the time, it never occurred to me how unusual it was for two divorced people, without children together, who never saw each other and lived such different lives, to spend so much time talking to each other.

When I came home alone for my father's funeral, this time after my deployment to Bahrain, I was a very different person. Although I didn't realize it at the time, I was mourning my separation from Alex, and I was more somber and not as prone to smile as I had once been. Nick came to my father's funeral alone, and he immediately noticed the change in me, assuming it was because of my father's death.

—Are you all right? he said. When I didn't answer him, he said, Your father was one of my heroes.

That had made me smile. I had reached over and hugged him. The feel of him, with my arms around him, made me cry. I'm not sure if I cried for myself or my father, but Nick took my hand.

—You want to come and see our new office spaces? It was such an unexpected thing for him to say that I laughed.

—Sure thing, I said. But first, I feel like I have to make an appearance at the reception at Cora's.

—Not a problem. I'll come, too, and afterwards, you can follow me out to the beach. That's where the offices are.

So, just like after my mother's funeral, we sat on Cora's terrace, talking to each other. He told me that the year before, he had formed a partnership with two other architects. The firm had purchased land and built a small office building, which, he proudly told me, blended into the landscape. Later, as he walked me through his work spaces, surrounded by floor to ceiling windows that looked out onto the marshlands of the Intercoastal Waterway, I thought that he had done really well for himself. I listened as he told me about the different projects they were involved with and their plans for the future, including expanding the work into consulting on large projects. He never said a single word about his wife or his three young sons. I figured their existence was in a different compartment of his life and something that he either didn't want to share with me or that he thought was outside of my area of interest. I didn't ask him about his family. All of our talk that day was entirely about our work.

Then right after I had retired and returned to Jacksonville, he had somehow heard I was back. He reached out to me to get together and have lunch. By that time, he was at the height of his career. His firm was involved in consulting for building projects all over the US, and he had become the face of the firm for these projects.

Now, ten years later, I was glad it was a good day for me. I had slept well the night before. It was truly miraculous what a good night's sleep could do for my mental acuity. I thought I looked as good as it was possible for me to look, with an emphasis on the not overweight part of my personal checklist. That was overly important to me for this meeting.

A part of my personality that went back to my formative years and my time with Nick was that I had always been concerned about not being overweight. Nick had always been fit and slim, the classic mesomorph, while I had always struggled with keeping my weight within the established weight standards for my height. I was an endomorph, like my father. The Marine Corps had handled this problem: either I kept within my weight limits or I would be processed out of the Marine Corps for not meeting weight standards. My twenty years in the Corps had kept me on the straight and narrow of weight control, keeping my weight at a steady 125 pounds, with a good bit of muscle tone, as well. My retirement had released those bonds, and with my new found freedom, I had gained twenty pounds. But, after twenty years of being fit, I couldn't help but feel that the extra weight reflected badly upon my self-discipline and self-worth. I had slowly but surely shed the weight, returning to only eating food that was good nutrition, and I started a regular exercise regime, as much for appearances as it was to keep my heart healthy. I was so relieved I looked slim.

This idea had not been in my mind when I had last seen Nick. At that time, I had just returned to Jacksonville. I hadn't stopped to consider how he even knew I was back. I had been caught up in the death of my sister Helen, and my mind was taken up with all things to do with her. The meeting was a quick touching base with an old acquaintance. This time I was fully in the moment, and I wanted to make sure I was my best self.

---

For our lunch, I drove to Jacksonville, to the Saint Johns Town Center, Jacksonville's version of an upscale, modern shopping mecca, with acres of shopping and restaurants. It took me over an hour to get there since it was almost to the beach, built on land once owned by dairy farmers.

During the drive, my internal jukebox decided to play Jackson Browne. I guessed this was because Jackson Browne had been Nick's favorite recording artist when we were in college. I remembered going over to his small apartment, just big enough for his bike, his bed, his clothes, his wall of speakers, and a turntable. Browne's album, *Late for the Sky*, had been played dozens and dozens and *dozens* of times. My mental jukebox played the song "Fountain of Sorrow" for me.

"Stop it!" I said out loud. I didn't want to be sad, to think about how our love had simply faded away. I didn't want to think about what a good and decent person he was and how I just up and left him. I didn't want to think about how this had made him feel. I didn't want to face up to the fact that I left him out of fear that the interesting, exciting part of my life with him was over, and that it was easier to leave and start fresh than to buckle down and figure out how to mature my relationship with him. There was also a lingering feeling that I hadn't been good enough for him, and that by leaving him, he had been prevented from ever leaving me. *Damn!* I thought, banging my hand on the steering wheel. *Get your shit together!* There was nothing I could do about it, and I had become a different person from the girl who had once loved him. I didn't want to let anything mar this luncheon date.

I turned on the radio, something I rarely did. This was because music with lyrics got stuck in my mind, playing over and over, after I turned it off. I decided to content myself with hip-hop music, something that I had never listened to, and I was hopeful that this fact would keep my mind from repeating what I heard after I turned the radio off. When I arrived at the restaurant, I locked my truck and paused to check my mind and see what was playing. I had been right: there were no hip-hop lyrics cycling through my mind like the lyrics bouncing on a screen at a karaoke bar.

Since I had about fifteen minutes before we were scheduled to meet, I ducked into the restroom of the high-end restaurant. I looked in the mirror while washing my hands, surprised I looked calm. I went back out to the reservation desk, telling the woman I was early, and asked if I could look at a menu and be seated. After she took me to a booth with comfortable leather seats, I took a moment to look around. The atmosphere was relaxing and inviting, with low lighting and fresh orchids on the tables. But this ambiance came with a price tag. When I opened up the menu to take a look, the price of lunch for two people was easily the same as my grocery bill for an entire week.

I had just finished looking it over when Nick came into the restaurant. Tall, slender, and clean-shaven, his once thick, dark-black hair was white, and he was bald on the top of his head. But, he was fit and healthy-looking, walking with a spring in his step and a smile on his face as he made his way to the table. Pictures of our life together passed before my eyes as he slid into the booth across from me and reached his hand across the table to squeeze mine. I smiled at him, meeting his gaze. The spark of attraction was no longer in that look; instead it was a friendly, open look, which told of someone who had achieved everything he had ever wanted to accomplish. But his eyes held something else. What it was I couldn't quite fathom.

—Nick! You look great!

—So do you, he said, holding my eyes for a second longer. He took his glasses out of their case, which he had put down on the table with his phone, and he picked up the menu.

—Well, how are you? I said.

—I'm good. Busy with work. And you?

—That wasn't just a question asked to be polite. I really want to know how you are, I said.

He looked up from the menu and his eyes softened.

—I'm a little tired. I'm not complaining, mind you. But, I've been traveling every week, primarily going back and forth to Charlotte. I nodded.

The waitress came over to our table.

—Do you know what you want? he said.

—I'll have whatever you're having. Since I had briefly looked over the menu, I knew there was nothing I couldn't or wouldn't eat, nothing spicy or unfamiliar.

—We'll have two steak Caesar salads. The server asked how we wanted the steak cooked, and he said, Rare.

—Not me, I said. Well-done. He looked at me, shaking his head and grinning. Just water to drink, I added.

—Same for me, he said. And, thanks.

Studying him as he talked to the waitress, I saw there was still a nobleness and handsomeness in his profile, but the look in his eyes still perplexed me. The waitress left and he looked back at me.

—Going back and forth to North Carolina? I said.

—Well, I should back up and tell you that we sold our firm last year to a big architectural firm in Boston.

—Wow! No kidding?

—Yeah, no kidding. He grinned. Since my two partners and I are about the same age, it was an offer that was too good to refuse. All three of us are working for the firm as consultants, at least for now, with the idea we'll all retire in the next couple of years.

—Good for you! He made it sound so easy. His consulting job was probably a compromise, a part of the give and take of the firm's sale, no doubt a complicated transaction. This job in Charlotte is part of your consulting work?

—Yes, but it was a job that my firm was already involved with when we sold it.

I listened as he told me about the job until the waitress brought out our lunches. In between bites, he told me about his developing friendship with the owner of the client company, which was primarily involved with the production of ammunition. I wasn't clear on what he did for this company, but I decided it didn't matter. It was just heartwarming to hear him talk. He had never been much of a talker when we were together. It wasn't that he was the strong and silent type, but he had never been one to wear out his welcome by talking too much. His talk was filled with his excitement over this project, and, as importantly I discerned, his feelings of parity with this billionaire who owned the company.

After we had finished eating and he had paid, we sat there, talking about what my sisters were doing, what his brother and sisters were up to these days, and what his sons were doing. I picked up on the fact that unlike Lizzy's daughter, his sons had no inclination to get married and start a family. And, there was no mention of his wife's activities.

—With your retirement only a couple of years away, do you have any plans? I said. He looked at me like I had asked him a question he hadn't even considered. I raised my eyebrows, saying, I had a boss once, a colonel, who used to say, "Always have a plan, but be willing to change it."

—Well, he said, Marge and I will probably travel some.
—All right. Any place in particular?
—Europe, I guess, he said, shrugging.
*He doesn't have any idea what he's going to do with the rest of his life,* I thought, saying,
—I can't tell you how good it was to hear about your success, Nick. You've achieved everything you've ever wanted. Those words were our cue to get up from the table, and we walked out together.
—I can't wait to see what you end up doing, I said as we said our good-byes out in front of the restaurant.
He looked at me. There was that look!. This time I recognized it. It was the look of fear. Not frightened-out-of-your-mind fear or the fear of losing something you valued but the most basic of human fears: fear of the unknown. His eyes said to me, loud and clear, *I am on the precipice of change, and what am I going to do with my life now?*
I reached out and hugged him, holding him longer than I meant to. It was a hug that said what I couldn't bring myself to say because it all sounded like platitudes: *Your life isn't over; it's just beginning. Something will present itself to you when you least expect it.* And I hoped the platitudes would turn out to be true. But hope is just wishful thinking, not something tangible to be harnessed.
On the drive home, my lunch with Nick had me thinking about how monetary wealth, more often than not, changes people, and if you're not careful, the changes are not for the better. Nick and I had no monetary wealth when we were married, but he was wealthy now, and I wondered whether it had changed him. I didn't like to think it had changed the essence of who he had been: aware of the health of the ocean and the beaches and concerned about leaving the planet in better shape than he had found it. But his work had moved him away from those youthful aspirations.

Aspirations did not provide for the things needed to survive in this world, but I liked to think he had prospered without completely abandoning his concern for the health of the planet.

He had never been one for material things, which had been one of his most attractive traits. When we were together, he drove an old white Plymouth sedan with a "Save the Whales" sticker on the rear bumper. His father gave the car to him, and he drove it the whole time we were married. He didn't have anything of value except for his stereo components and his surfboards. And, his clothes were basic: work clothes, a couple pairs of jeans, T-shirts, shorts, and his baggies for surfing.

Now, he drove a top-of-the-line Range Rover, his clothes, while understated, were obviously expensive, and I understood from my sisters that he lived in a multimillion dollar home at Atlantic Beach. I didn't remember Nick ever saying he wanted to be wealthy, and I liked to think it was just a reflection of his professional success. Since I hadn't liked his wife, she was the perfect candidate on which to lay the blame for the more obvious signs of Nick's wealth, though he had every right to buy whatever he chose with his money.

But it wasn't the money he had that made him happy. It was a side benefit. He loved being an architect. He had always had his heart set on that profession, and he had done better than he ever could have imagined. But, for Nick, now in his sixties, the work would be over soon. And without a plan to exit that existence onto the highway of something else, he seemed lost. What now?

I sent a message out into the great universe: *Peace and joy to Nick, and may he find his way to something fulfilling as he transitions to this next phase of his life.* There was nothing else I could do, and he deserved the best wishes I could send him. He was such a kind and good person, even if he hadn't been very good in the choice of his wives.

# Ku'u Lei Awapuhi

I had just finished polishing my mother's silver after having cleaned her fine China, the early November steps in my Thanksgiving marathon of hosting my family for the holiday, and was getting ready to take the girls for a walk when the phone rang. Picking it up, I was happy to see the name Katrina Swiftwater, on the screen.

Over the decades, thanks to Kat, we had remained friends. Our friendship stretched back to my days as a public defender in Jacksonville. When she and I had worked together, she had been head over heels in love with one of the most dynamic and successful criminal defense attorneys in the city. But as always seems to happen with those sorts of people, he attracted admirers, and one night she came home to find him with one of them in flagrante delicto. She moved back home to Montana, and went to work for the federal public defender in Billings. There she met Phil, another high-powered criminal defense attorney, but this one was a woman, Phillipa, ten years older than Kat, who was my age.

Kat was one of those wonderful people whom I believed to be more evolved than most. Part of it was her bisexuality. She had the ability to love someone, male or female, with an all-encompassing love: physical, mental, and spiritual. I believed the spiritual aspect of her love was tied to her Cherokee heritage. And, she was also evolved in the nature of her friendship. When she decided she was your friend, it was for life. Throughout my years in the Marine Corps, she always kept up with me, no matter where I was or what was going on in our lives.

When I thought of her, I was usually reminded of a trip she, Phil, Matt, and I took together for a week of sailing off Key West. That trip was over-the-top wonderful. The four of us took turns preparing meals on the thirty-foot sailboat we had rented, and Phil made her delicious pupu platters, food she had grown up eating in Maui. Matt, a lover of all things Hawaiian, was in heaven. The laughs and interesting talks we had, as well as the circus-like atmosphere surrounding our getting stuck on a shallow reef, and the hoops Phil and Matt had to jump through to get the boat loose had, over time, lent this trip a mythic quality in my memory.

Picking up the phone, I said,

—Kat! It's so good to hear from you!

—Julie, she said, sounding like she was crying.

—What's wrong? I said, immediately concerned.

—It's Phil. She died yesterday, she said, sounding, literally, heartbroken.

As she talked to me, the tears streamed down my face. She told me that the morning before, she had woken up early for her yoga class, and she had quietly left the room so as not to wake Phil. She thought she had left her sleeping. When she came home, Phil wasn't in the kitchen, watching the news and eating breakfast. When she went into their bedroom looking for her, her body was already cold.

—She looked peaceful, so relaxed, looking like if I just shook her hard enough she would wake up.

—I'm so sorry. Is there anything I can do?

—No, Julie, nothing. It's just good to have someone to talk to about it, and I thought you would want to know. My sister drove over yesterday from Grand Forks. She's going to stay for a while and help me arrange the cremation once the body is returned to me. Since Phil died in her sleep, they have to do an autopsy to make sure she died of natural causes.

She said this like it was just something to be done before the cremation, but I thought it said something about our society. Phil had been in her mid-seventies. She and Kat were married, having tied the knot in 2014 when same-sex marriage was legalized across the US. Since Phil had been wealthy, she didn't feel the need for life insurance, but society didn't trust that wealthy people died naturally, in their sleep.

—Do you have any idea what she died from? I said.

—I'm thinking it was something with her heart. She hadn't had much energy lately, complaining of fatigue, saying that her mind felt foggy. She thought it was just because she had been tired, working as a consultant on this case involving the local police.

—That makes sense. When will you know something?

—Next week. The coroner's office said they will let me know when the autopsy is completed.

I felt an irrational concern for Kat's well-being, perhaps because she always felt everything intensely, love and hate, happiness and sadness. She and Phil had been inseparable soulmates. They reminded me of Lizzy and Josh but without children. When I had been around them, it was sometimes difficult to figure out where one person ended and the other began, a "we" entity rather than two "I's." They seemed to have an innate ability to communicate without speaking.

—I'm worried your grief is going to be as great as your love. Will you call me if it gets to be too much?

—I'm okay, really, she said. Having Di here with me right now helps. We've always been close, so I'm not alone. But thanks.

—Good! I said, relieved.

She started talking about the plans she and Phil had made for the next year: their annual National Geographic trip, this time to Egypt, and their annual trip up into the Rocky Mountains to camp and fish.

—I don't want to have any type of ceremony to commemorate her life until next spring, Kat said. It's too cold here to do anything outside.

—Well, you'll have some time to think about what you really want to do.

—I need to feel the sun, she said. I want to come to Florida... to our place on Manasota Key. Can you come and see me?

—Of course I can! I said, trying to keep track of her racing mind as it moved from one seemingly unrelated topic to the next.

Kat and Phil owned a small house on the beautiful eleven-mile-long barrier island south of Sarasota. Although they didn't come every year, whenever they had come to escape the cold, I always made the trip to stay a couple of days with them.

—It will be good to see you, she said, sounding to me like she was floating on the ocean, alone, after her boat had sunk, with no life preserver in sight.

—I love you, Kat, I said, feeling so helpless. Thanks for calling me and letting me know.

—Love you, too, she said. See you soon.

---

In early December, I drove the little over three hours it took to reach Kat's place on the barrier island of Manasota Key. The first time I had been to this area of the Gulf coast was when Matt and I had gone there to get married on Sanibel Island thirty years ago. It had been a sleepy little tucked-away area of the state, but it was no longer sleepy. The Tampa Bay area had expanded down to Sarasota, so I couldn't tell when I'd left one town and was entering another. When I drove across the causeway to get to Manasota, it was still beautiful despite all the development. I made my way to Kat's place, off of Beach Road.

She heard my truck pull up and came out the front door to greet me. Slender and statuesque, her thick, waist-length, formerly jet-black hair was now silver, pulled back and loosely braided. Her face looked like a female version of Sitting Bull's: fine wrinkles, dark intelligent-looking eyes, and those beautiful cheek bones and slim, straight nose. She hugged me tightly, and I responded, feeling how thin she had gotten since the last time I had seen her.

—The first thing we need to do is go to the grocery store and get some food. You need to eat, I said, surprising myself. I wasn't one to mother people, but something about Kat's situation made me want to take care of her.

—I haven't felt like eating, she said.

—I know, I said, even though I didn't know what she was feeling. But, if you continue to pine away for Phil, you'll be joining her sooner rather than later. I reached up and tucked a loose hair behind her right ear. I don't want that to happen. Come on. I'm hungry. Let me take my things in the house, and then let's go get something to eat before we go to the grocery store. Okay?

—Okay, she said. I squeezed her hand. I got my overnight bag out of the truck, and we walked into her house, chatting about my drive down.

We drove to Kat and Phil's favorite place to eat, a small restaurant with a covered seating area and bar in the back. There were about ten barstools, each one occupied, everybody drinking and talking and laughing. The parrot in a floor-to-ceiling cage behind the bar was very Jimmy Buffetesque. Bright green and yellow, it was constantly moving back and forth on its perch, taking in the activity in the room and saying, "Pieces of eight," "Love you darlin'," and "Ho, ho, ho." I thought perhaps they hadn't taught the parrot to complete the sentence with "and a bottle of rum," but maybe the parrot just didn't want to say it.

After we ordered, fresh-caught shrimp and salads for each of us, I filled the space left by Kat's silence with talk of everything I had been doing with the lake place.

—That's all I'm going to say," I said, finally. I want to hear about how you're doing. No bullshit, okay?

—I'm hanging in there, she said, but I scared myself.

—Scared yourself? I said, worried.

—Yeah, she said, nodding. After I heard from the coroner that Phil had died of a massive heart attack, the body was returned to me, and we had Phil cremated. My sister went back home to her family, leaving me in that big house, all alone. All I did was wander from one room to another, crying. I didn't know how I was going to live without her. Then one morning, I caught a glimpse of myself in the bathroom mirror. I didn't recognize my face. It looked like a death mask. That morning, I went to my yoga class for the first time since her death. It saved my life. I nodded, and she said, Julie, I mean it. Just going to that class and feeling the energy and power of yoga practice as it seeped into my body made me realize I wanted to live. Ever since then, I have just been taking it one day at a time. I go to yoga practice every day now, and I'm thinking about starting Pilates, too.

—That's not a bad idea, I said, but, if you plan on starting Pilates, you're going to have to eat. I mean really eat. You've always been one of those lucky people who never had to worry about getting fat. That fact's not your friend right now. Especially if you're going to start doing a potentially intensive form of exercise, like Pilates.

—I know, she said, smiling at me for the first time.

—Oh, Kat! It's so good to see you smile. What do you say let's go for a walk on the beach when we get back from the grocery store? Maybe we'll find some pretty shells.

—I would like that, she said, reaching across the table with both of her hands to take mine, squeezing them.

Later that evening, I fixed her a power shake made with fruit and whole-milk yogurt. She drank it without complaint as we sat out in her backyard, a small area shaded during the daytime by palm trees. The gorgeous bougainvillea, dark red and pink, created a real feel of privacy. We talked about our siblings. For Christmas, Kat was planning a trip to see her older brother, who lived in Panama. He had left the United States five years ago, deciding to become an expat, tired of the press of the population in California. I could relate to his feeling of the need for space. She told me about Panama; she and Phil had gone to see him last year, having rented a place near the beach for the three months they visited him. I asked her about Phil's brother, a psychiatrist. He had worked at Tripler Army Medical Center in Honolulu when I met him. For the two weeks I was at Tripler after my stroke, he checked in on me every day and continued checking on me even after I had been released to return to work. He and his wife were devastated by Phil's death, and Kat said he was always checking on her, too. With the talk of Phil's brother, her face saddened.

—Every time I think of her, I feel so lonely. The grieving therapist I have been going to has told me this is very normal. Grief is a form of loneliness, you know.

—That makes sense, I said. You're seeing a therapist?

—My sister insisted. Di was adamant, threatening to come live with me if I didn't start seeing someone to help me cope.

—Good sister. Is it helping?

—I think so. Knowing that other people have felt the way I do helps. I'm not sure why. But it just does.

After we went back inside and said our good nights, I sat in bed reading one of the three-year-old magazines that were on the bedside table. Kat knocked and opened the door.

—I can't sleep. My mind won't shut down.

I patted the empty side of the queen-sized bed.

—You can sleep with me, if you want to. I don't think I snore, I said, smiling broadly.

She smiled back at me and came over, slipping under the covers. As I turned off the light, she scooted over near me.

—Would you like me to put my arm around you? I said.

—Would you mind?

—Of course not, I said, pulling my pillow over, putting my right arm around her waist, and making myself comfortable.

—Sometimes Phil's snoring was so loud, I had to get up and go sleep in the guest room. But, since I always woke up before she did, I came and got back in bed before she woke up. I don't think she ever knew.

—Did she always snore? Or was it just something she did as she got older?

—She always snored, especially when she was tired and hadn't had much sleep, like when she had been in court for days on end. But, in the last two years or so, she snored really loud, every night. I miss that now. Before, it was just something I put up with.

—I understand that, I said. And I did. Although neither Nick nor Matt had snored, Alex had.

Within five minutes, she was sound asleep. I didn't want to move and wake her. I relaxed, breathing and thinking about my dogs. Lizzy had come to stay with them, so I wasn't worried, but I did miss them. They were good companions, and since I had gotten them, one month apart, when I returned to Jacksonville, I had never felt lonely. Even though they were probably enjoying their time with Lizzy, they would be overjoyed when I returned.

With my mind in a happy place, I was soon fast asleep.

When I woke up the next morning, Kat was gone. I could hear her out in the kitchen and smelled the aroma of frying bacon.

—Smells wonderful! I said, as I walked into the kitchen. I haven't had bacon in ages.

—It was our tradition to have a big breakfast the first morning we arrived here. I always cooked eggs, pancakes, and bacon, and I juiced fresh oranges. I didn't feel like doing it by myself yesterday.

The table looked like a staged photo for a magazine: scrambled eggs, thick cut strips of perfectly browned bacon, a stack of pancakes with the butter melting over the sides, and a clear pitcher full of juice, the pulp mixed in, looking like a citrus snow globe.

—I had forgotten what a great cook you are, I said, sitting down at the breakfast bar and pouring myself a large cup of coffee from the carafe.

—Phil loved my cooking, she said, with a sadness that now tinged her voice whenever she talked of her partner.

—Yes, she did! I said, thinking of Phil. She had been a big-boned and tall woman. Her mother had been Polynesian, and Phil had the thick dark hair, large dark eyes, and perpetually sun-tanned-looking skin of the Hawaiian people. Never what you would call slender, as she had gotten older, she had gotten heavy. And, she had been bigger-than-life; one of those bright and exciting people who charmed you into their orbit as if by a gravitational pull.

—Come on, I said, motioning her to sit down and eat.

—I'm not really hungry, she said, pouring herself a glass of orange juice.

—Oh, yes you are! I said, taking a plate and putting on it a little bit of everything she had put out for me. Eat, just a little. Please . . . for me.

She sighed and sat down.

—Where did you get this cute pitcher? I said as we ate. The small pink pitcher, now filled with maple syrup, was only large enough to hold about eight ounces. It was shaped like a flamingo and glazed with a shiny paint, making it glow.

—Micki . . . Micki Lowenstein gave it to me when she came to visit us last year.

—How is she? I said. Micki was a lawyer we had worked with in the public defender's office in Jacksonville. A couple of years older than we were, she was a high-energy, dedicated defense counsel.

—She hasn't changed a bit, she said, a small smile crossing her face. She was all up in arms about that article in *The New Yorker* magazine.

—What article? I said, pouring maple syrup over my pancakes.

—You don't know? Oh, Julie, I'm sorry! I just assumed you would know about it. The one about Matt.

—I have no idea what you're talking about, I said, looking over at her, stunned.

She got up from the table and went into her bedroom to get her phone. She pulled up the feature article in the magazine, dated last year, and handed it over to me to read. It detailed the CIA's efforts to hang Matt out to dry after he blew the whistle on the undisclosed use of CIA information in FBI investigations into drug smuggling.

—Matt was always interested in the truth, I said, after finishing the article. He was a stickler for fairness and transparency in the cases he prosecuted. I'm proud of him. It's tough playing with the big boys.

—It is, she said. That's what Micki was going on and on about after she showed us the article. Even though, as she said, Matt went over to the dark side, meaning the prosecution, she admitted that he was the type of prosecutor she thought only existed in her dreams: one that was honest, wanted to get to the truth of the matter, and believed in the American system of justice.

—I wonder what Matt would think of that. Micki and Matt never got along. I can remember an argument they had in the hallway of the PD's office. It drew a crowd.

—I remember, said Kat, now grinning, all thoughts of Phil gone for a second. Do you remember what it was about?

—Not really, I said. All I remember is that the argument caused such a ruckus that Patrick Black had to get in between the two of them to make sure it didn't come to blows. This was before Matt and I started dating. You know, I've never worked with the FBI or the CIA. When I think of FBI agents, I think of Johnny Utah.

—Who's Johnny Utah, she said, looking at me, clueless.

—You don't know who Johnny Utah is? Have you never seen *Point Break*, the movie with Keanu Reeves and Patrick Swayze?

—No, why?

—You need to see it. It's a classic. Matt and I went to see it when it was released, when we were living on Okinawa. But, essentially, Johnny Utah, played by Keanu Reeves, is a young FBI agent. At his first job in LA, he's part of the armed robbery unit. His partner believes the serial armed robbers they're trying to catch are surfers. Patrick Swayze plays one of the surfers, called Bodhi, short for Bodhisattva. I won't tell you anything else because I don't want to ruin it for you. Anyway, that's how I've pictured FBI agents, looking for the truth. But, I realize real FBI agents are just people, with issues, compounded by the fact they're at the top of the law enforcement food chain. And they probably don't look like a young Keanu Reeves.

—No, she said, looking serious. They don't. The ones I dealt with were older, seasoned law enforcement officers. There aren't any stupid FBI agents. It's tough to get into the FBI, and you have to be smart to survive in that organization.

—The article inferred, I said, that the FBI was using the CIA information to help increase their funding.

—That may have been part of it. The FBI agents I knew were true believers. They believed their job was to make sure all criminals were captured and punished. The end always justifies the means. Very Machiavellian.

—Matt never liked people who didn't play fair, I said. Kat nodded. The article also said he was made a scapegoat, wasn't treated like a protected whistleblower, and was someone for DOJ to point the finger at, so they could smooth over their relationship with the CIA and the FBI.

—Sounded that way to us, too, Kat said. Micki had been doing some checking around to try to find out what happened to him.

—Did she find out anything?

—Well, she found out he's living in Hawaii now, working at the US Attorney's office there, and that he's remarried.

—I'm glad! I said, relieved at this news. I wonder how he met her? Although it doesn't really matter. All that matters is he's in Hawaii, and that he has someone to love him.

—You're really happy for him? she asked, looking skeptical.

—Of course I am. I know I've never talked about our divorce. It was too painful to talk about. But, with the passing of time, it's easier for me to own up to the fact that it was my fault.

—Your fault?

—Yes, my fault. Our relationship had become strained by my jobs. I was fortunate—or perhaps unfortunate—enough to have high profile jobs, which took most of my time and energy. Plus, he didn't want to live anywhere else but Hawaii. That fact was like a line drawn in the sand.

—And when I got orders to Bahrain and fell in love with a man I met there, it was the end of the road for our marriage.

—You've never told me about this man before, she said.

—I know. Our relationship was something I couldn't talk about—he was in the Marine Corps, too. There would have been repercussions if anyone found out about our affair.

—What kind of repercussions?

—Like both of us kicked out of the Marine Corps repercussions, I said. When I say it out loud, it sounds so antiquated, but the military is all about having rules, and adultery is prohibited. Plus, an affair, when we were deployed, both senior officers, wouldn't have been something that could be easily over-looked, or chalked up to the unusual circumstances in which we found ourselves. Very bad juju.

—Bad juju?

— It means the karmic consequences of an action, I said. And for whatever reason, it's a popular saying in the military.

—Interesting, she said.

—And then when I had the stroke, I had the whole healing process to deal with. The idea of ever talking to you about it was moved to the back burner.

I got up and began clearing off the table.

—I would never know you had a stroke to look at you now, she said.

—I never thought about the workings of the mind before I had one, I said. The mind is beyond amazing. After the stroke, the neurologist told me I'd have to get used to the idea that I wasn't as smart as I used to be. That's true but I like to tell myself that I'm a better person now. It's like I woke up from my self-centered dream. But, I wish I was more like you. When you love someone you never stop loving them. Fearless love, I call it. You've always been fearless.

—You think I'm fearless? she said. I'm afraid all the time now.

—You're grieving, I said, coming up behind her and putting

my arms around her neck. One day you're going to wake up and feel whole again. But, when you do, don't feel guilty! You'll always love Phil, and that love is something you'll always have. I know, I know, I'm preaching! I'll shut up now!
 She turned her head to look at me.
 —I hope you're right.
 —I am, I said, making myself sound surer than I felt. I looked at the kitchen clock over her head; it was eight thirty. I squeezed her, kissed her on the top of her head, took my arms from around her neck and went to finish clearing off the table.
 —So, who's coming next?
 —Di and her daughter, Jessica, are flying in tonight. They've never been here before, and my niece has a list of all the things she wants to do while she's here.
 —But, that's good, right? I said.
 —I suppose so, she said, looking like she wasn't sure about that at all.
 —Come on, let's go for a walk on the beach before everybody else gets out there, I said. I want to get on the road before lunchtime.
 I had always adhered to the expression attributed to Benjamin Franklin: guests, like fish, begin to smell after three days. Kat knew that was my modus operandi when I came for a visit. We finished cleaning up, got dressed, and headed to the beach.

---

 On my drive home, my mental jukebox decided to play songs by Hapa. The name of the group, a word meaning "half" in Hawaiian, came from the two front men in the band, one Hawaiian and one Caucasian. I thought their music was melodic, the voices of the men blending together so beautifully. I didn't understand the words, as most of the songs were sung in the Hawaiian language, but my mind sang them anyway.

Matt had loved listening to them. I pulled over at the next gas station, fired up Apple CarPlay, and found their albums on my phone. Making an exception to my normal rule about listening to music while I was driving, I started playback and pulled back onto the road. With the real music playing, my mental jukebox was silent. While I listened, I thought about Matt and his love of Hawaii.

He had loved it from the very first time he had visited there, back when we were public defenders and had been sent to a CLE conference out there for a week. He had become addicted to Hawaii on that first visit. It was as if he fell in love with it. I remembered he spent every minute he could, soaking up the feel of the Big Island.

The second time we had gone there was for a vacation when we were stationed on Okinawa. It rained the whole time, but he didn't care. He was happy for the entire trip, dragging me from one place to the next to taste the food and to see the different tourist sites on Maui.

Four years later, he decided that he didn't want to remain in the Marine Corps. He had worked with the US Attorney's office in Virginia as a military prosecutor of the civilians who had committed crimes aboard Marine Corps Base Quantico, and he felt that the job as a US Attorney was a better fit for him. But, overarching everything, he had wanted to live in Hawaii, and I had used my position as the adjutant of the barracks to obtain orders there.

While living there, he had immersed himself in its culture, learned to surf, and had become a valued member of a Hawaiian outrigger team. When I received orders to return to Washington, he didn't want to leave. And it was only later, that he had reluctantly joined me, briefly taking a job with the Department of

Justice in DC. But, he was like a fish out of water. That's the way I thought about it. When I again used my position to obtain orders to return to Hawaii, he left months ahead of me, anxious to return "home."

Throughout our marriage, Matt's love of Hawaii and his need to be there colored our life together. I thought now that his love of Hawaii was like my love of the lake. It was part of his soul, his true home. I hoped he could find some contentment now that he lived there. I hoped he was still physically able to surf, something he had taken to so naturally. But, more than anything else, I prayed to the great universe that he was truly happy with his life.

# I Want to Know What Love is

At eight thirty in the morning on Christmas Eve, the phone rang.
—Jules, it's Steve McBride.
—Steve, I said, putting down my cup of coffee. This is such a nice surprise! What's up?
—Jules, he said, sounding somber, I called because I wanted to tell you about Alex before you found out from someone else.
I felt like he had just knocked all the air out of my lungs, and I felt a pressure bring tears to my eyes.
—I'm not sure how to tell you, other than to just say it. Alex died in an avalanche in the Alps. The one that made the news a week ago. Did you hear about it?
I didn't respond immediately.
—Jules, are you still there?
I nodded my head, my vision clouded from the tears. I brushed them away, saying.
—I'm here, and, no, I didn't hear anything about the avalanche. And . . . good for him.
—What? he said, sounding astonished.
—What I mean is that Alex didn't want to be an old man. I assume he was skiing, so he died doing what he loved to do best.

There was silence on the line. Steve?

—I'm here . . . and well . . . you're right.

Alex had always been the elephant in the room between us. Steve and I had become friends separate and apart from my relationship with Alex, Steve's best friend at the time. We were not close, but I did consider him a friend, centered on the intensity of the life we had shared in Bahrain at MARCENT. We had never shared our close secrets, but over the years, he and I had made it a point to talk to each other during the year, to text each other occasionally, and always wished each other happy birthday on the Marine Corps' birthday. Now, with him telling me that Alex had died, the elephant in the room had vanished.

—I didn't mean to sound callous and unfeeling, I said, steeling myself not to break down and cry, holding on for all I was worth. He was an incredible person. You should know that I always envied your friendship. He told me about how you two became friends.

—He did?

—Yes, he did, I said. And how you took him under your wing. Those are the exact words he used, "took me under his wing." You befriended him, believed in him, and, really, he believed you were instrumental in saving his career. Because he trusted you and felt like he could tell you pretty much anything, I figured he must have told you about the liaison or relationship or whatever you want to call it that he and I had in Bahrain.

—No, Jules, he said, slowly. He never told me outright. But, somehow I knew. I don't know how, exactly, and if anyone had asked me to prove it, I wouldn't have been able to, but I knew, and that's one of the reasons I called you. You were the first person I thought of when I got off the phone with his sister yesterday.

He was silent for a moment, then continued.

—When he came to work with me for the G-5 at I MEF, he

and I never directly talked about why he was there. He got a raw deal, what with being removed from his position as the executive officer of Third Battalion. Word was that his commanding officer was arrogant, brash, and not really the sharpest tool in the shed, if you know what I mean.

—I do, I said.

—Eventually, Third Battalion's CO was relieved of command for mistreatment of subordinates, but, by that time, Alex had been gone from the battalion for about six months. The G-5 at the time felt the way I did about Alex's abilities, and he made sure on Alex's fitness report to try to right any wrongs that had been done to him. But, even though he had commands as a lieutenant colonel and a colonel, he never was given command of a battalion.

—It's strange, I said, but it seemed like the command he had as a lieutenant colonel in North Africa was a better fit for his personality than an infantry battalion.

—Isn't that the truth! Steve said, a smile in his voice. But, there was something else I wanted to talk to you about.

—What's that?

—The phone call from his sister yesterday.

—This was his half-sister, Cynthia?

—Cynthia was her name, but I didn't know she was his half-sister.

—Not that it matters, but his mother had been previously married. She's five or six years older, and Alex told me that he and his sister never got along. He felt like she resented the fact that he even existed. Plus, he said she didn't care for his father, and that the only reason he had anything to do with her was because of his mother.

—That's interesting, he said. Did he tell you anything else about her?

—Well, the only other thing that comes to mind is that she

made like she was devastated, even though she wasn't, when his father died. This was when Alex was in his first year of college. From what I understand, she still lived at home with their mother. And, come to think of it, I believe she was living with his mother when we were in Bahrain.

—That sheds a little light on our conversation, he said, thoughtfully. I was shocked when she told me Alex had died skiing. She didn't seem upset about his death but was upset that—unbeknownst to me—he had made me the executor of his will. She was adamant that I should pass the executor's responsibilities over to her.

—What did you say?

—I didn't know what to say. His death was such a shock. I told her that I didn't know anything about it and asked her how she knew. She told me his lawyer had told her when he had called her that morning. She finally gave me his number but not until I told her I couldn't make any decisions until I talked to the lawyer.

—You talked to him?

—Yeah. He seemed like a good enough guy, saying he was glad I called, and apologized I had found out about Alex's death from his sister. He never expected her to call me, and he hadn't given her my phone number. He said after he finished letting all the family members on Alex's contact sheet know of his death, he was going to call me. But more importantly, he told me that there wouldn't be any problem in me carrying out my duties from here.

—Steve, you could turn executorship over to his lawyer and wash your hands of it.

—No, Jules, I can't. Alex wanted me to do it. His lawyer also told me he left everything to a woman named Alicia Fairbanks and her son, Christian. Do you know who they are?

—No idea, I said. Curiouser and curiouser.

—And Jules, because of the avalanche, they haven't recovered his body yet. The avalanche was massive; hundreds of feet of snow collapsed down onto the slope of the mountain. That's another thing his lawyer told me. I'm guessing they will dig his body out soon, but I'm not really sure how that works. I've never had any reason to think about avalanches before. I'm strictly a warm-weather person.

—So am I. Although I did try to learn how to snowboard after I met Alex. He had told me so much about his love of the snow that I felt like I had to experience it. There definitely was a beauty to it, especially the deep quiet of those winter places. But, Steve, do you know who's going to plan the funeral?

—I asked his lawyer about that, too. He told me Alex specified cremation in his will and that he wanted to have his ashes spread on the Tetons. Both his parents are dead, and since he didn't leave his sister anything, I don't think she'll be interested in making those kind of arrangements. I'll talk to his lawyer again after the holidays, but the bottom line is I don't know. I may end up doing it myself.

—It shouldn't be difficult. My dad's brother had his ashes scattered in the foothills of the Smokey Mountains. Everybody took a handful of ashes, said a few words, and then released them into the light wind. It was so peaceful.

—I've never thought about taking care of my funeral arrangements, he said. But, it's something I need to do.

—Me, too, I said. But, Steve, thank you for calling me and letting me know. Really.

After I got off the phone, I headed back into the kitchen to get another cup of coffee. Then, I went over to the cabinet in the living room to raid my stash of chocolate, a large bag of Dove dark chocolate. Since I no longer drank alcohol, and I had never used drugs, it was my only go-to vice for consoling myself. As I drank the very dark, very strong coffee and ate my dark chocolate breakfast, I thought about Alex's death. Over the last fifteen years, as his face had slowly faded from my mind and the sound of his voice no longer reverberated in my ears, my strongest memory of him had taken on the role of a talisman: the feel of him behind me, his soft kisses on my neck and shoulders, his arms around me as we lay in his bed, spent from having made love far into the night. This talisman was one that I leaned on when I needed emotional support or combated self-pity, and I used it like a shield to keep negative feelings at bay.

I put down my coffee cup and put the bag of chocolate back in the cabinet. I called to the girls, put on my fleece-lined jacket, and we went out onto the porch. Above the trees, a cloudless sky had started to lighten. Mist rose from the lake as the cold air met the warmer water, and the early morning fog blanketed the other side of the lake. This was the first really cold day of December, and the air was crisp with the promise of a truly beautiful winter day.

As they went out into the yard, I stood there, thinking, leaning on the ledge surrounding the porch, looking out across the lake. I had always felt like I left a piece of my soul behind me, with him, when I left Bahrain. I had never been able to move on with my life or to harden my heart and turn my back on our time together. There had been a time when I had missed him so much that it almost hurt, physically.

One night in Hawaii, the moon was so bright that its light woke me up in the middle of the night. I went out onto the lanai and just stood there, staring up at the moon. It seemed impossibly large, its wide reflection stretching out across Kāneʻohe Bay to the Pacific Ocean. Without thinking about it, I reached out my hand to cover the moon saying, "I hope life is good to you. Be safe." For me, that night, my hand over the moon, was a supplication to the moon to watch over Alex in Bahrain.

After my stroke, this simple act had taken on a life of its own.

I had simply needed something positive to keep my head above water. I had blocked out what the rational side of my brain knew: Alex was someone who I didn't have much in common with and whose ultraconservative politics were at the opposite end of the scale from mine. He was someone who listened to Rush Limbaugh every weekend and, as far as I knew, concurred with his views and was not just listening to him for entertainment value. Plus, I knew he was an introvert, accustomed to being on his own. He wasn't someone who you would call kind, like Nick; and he didn't think to ask me what I thought about things or how I felt about things, like Matt. My rational mind knew that loving someone like Alex didn't make good sense for me. But, the romantic side of my mind had this vision of Alex as Superman, cape ruffling in the breeze, as he stood atop the Empire State Building. This side of my mind focused on his intelligence, his fearlessness, and his physical beauty. Nobody could outthink him, nothing frightened him, and his masculine beauty called out to be touched. But, his most important quality was that being with him had made me feel safe, and I had thought of him as my sanctuary. And he treated me like a rare and beautiful creature, something I had never experienced before I met him.

I recalled that he had once used the expression "like two ships passing in the night" to describe us. At the time, I had not given that statement much thought. But, now I knew it was used to describe people who meet for a short, intense period and then do not see each other again. He always knew our time together would be brief, ending as quickly as it had begun.

It had been the most extraordinary time of my life, a time when I thought I could die without feeling that I had missed out on the best of what life had to offer. And, my time in Bahrain was a period of my life with a lot of good memories. The primary maker of those memories would never see that beautiful full moon again, shining bright in the sky, looking so close that he might feel it was within reach.

I was starting to feel cold, so I called to the girls, and followed them back inside. I went and got my laptop, and getting comfortable on the couch, I typed into the search engine "recent avalanche in the Alps." I clicked on an article from CNN.

The short article said this particular one had been 2,500-feet-wide, hundreds of feet deep, and took place in the Bernese Alps. The two skiers who were confirmed missing were not identified. And, the missing skiers, the first to ski down, triggering the avalanche in their wake, were in a party of nine, including a mountain guide. The article focused on how experienced this group of skiers was, with particular emphasis on the fact that the mountain guide had consulted the most recent avalanche bulletin. Evidently, this bulletin was published when there was heavy snowfall, and it had been taken into account before the group ascended. Plus, everybody was equipped with avalanche transceivers. It pointed out that every safety precaution had been taken but noted there was always the risk of an avalanche on very steep slopes, this one being particularly steep. I'm sure that the steepness of the slope was part of the thrill for Alex. I hoped the snow came down on him before he had time to think about it; the sheer power and weight of the snow knocking him unconscious, enveloping him quickly, and burying him deep. I could think of no other way he would have rather died.

After reading a couple more articles about the avalanche, I decided to find out what an avalanche transceiver was used for. It sounded like it was something used to help locate a person trapped under the snow, and I found out I had guessed right. I figured it probably wouldn't be too long, winter or not, before his body was located. In the new year, I would check back with Steve to see if he had heard anything.

Later that morning, I saw Lars's truck pull into his lot across the street. I hurried into the kitchen and filled a holiday cookie tin with an assortment of the Christmas cookies I had made to give to my family the next day. Then, I headed across the street to talk to him.

He had returned from Michigan in early November, and I hadn't had any contact with him, except the occasional wave, since we had dinner at my place before he left for his trip. With the Christmas season upon us, I figured that it would be a good time to apologize for my unfriendly behavior.

—Lars, happy holidays! I said, as he came out of his storage building. I have some Christmas cookies for you.

He smiled at me and took the tin. I took a deep breath.

—And, I want to apologize for my behavior. I didn't know how to tell you that I wasn't interested in any kind of a romantic relationship. Not that I'm suggesting you were either. It made me uncomfortable, so I just shut down. I'm sorry. Of course, we never talked about it, but I'm still in love with someone else. And, I had the impression you're still in love with your wife, too.

Listening to me, a look of hopelessness appeared in his eyes, and his expression turned sad. I realized that my words had caught him off guard.

—I've been dating a woman, he said, sounding like that was something he had to do rather than something he enjoyed doing. I met her in Melrose at the live music sessions they have there at the outside pavilion on the weekends. She's divorced and lives in Waldo. I've helped her out by refinishing her kitchen, and she wants me to help her with one of the bathrooms next. But, you know, I don't think the relationship is going anywhere.

—You'll never know unless you ask her, I said.

He looked at me as if I had lost my mind.

I smiled.

—Well, let's not be strangers, okay? I said.

—Of course not. And thank you for the cookies. Merry Christmas!

I turned, waving good-bye, on my way back across the street. I hoped that Lars would find a way to work through his grief. It occurred to me that fear was mixed up with his grief: fear that he would never meet anyone who would love him the way his wife had loved him. Part of me wanted to tell him that he wouldn't, and the sooner he recognized that and made peace with that, the easier it would be for him. But, Lars didn't need my opinion, because it was none of my business. Perhaps someday he and I would be friends, but not today. And, what I had just told him was true. I couldn't understand it or rationalize it, but I hoped I would always love Alex. Love was like a drink of water when you were parched. It was the be-all and end-all of everything. To die without ever having been in love was a fate that I'd been spared. That was a fact I could chalk up in the positive column of life's ups and downs. As I walked back to my house, my mind put money in my mental jukebox, deciding to play Foreigner's "I Want to Know What Love Is."

I woke up the next morning, with a decision made: when I called Steve to find out if they had recovered Alex's body, I would tell him that, when he set a date to spread Alex's ashes, I wanted to go.

---

Four months later, I was in the airport at Jackson, Wyoming, waiting on Steve's plane to arrive from its Chicago layover. Never having been there before, I had read up on the place in preparation for my trip and learned that Jackson, at the south end of Jackson Hole, was an iconic town of the American West. The term

"Hole" referred to a large valley surrounded by mountains. A placard at the airport informed me that the two mountain ranges in question were called by Canadian fur traders "Les Trois Tétons," or the three nipples, and "Gros Ventre," the French name for an Algonquian-speaking Indian tribe, which was native to Montana.

I took a walk around to stretch my legs and strolled through the shops, finally getting some coffee and finding a seat near Steve's arrival gate in front of windows that looked out across the runway to the mountains' snow-covered beauty. Watching the travelers, I thought many of the adults, young and old, reminded me of the characters Neo, Trinity, and Morpheus of *The Matrix* fame, wearing their dark glasses inside the airport, looking around them as if everybody were a lesser race of creatures and not fellow travelers on their way toward death. Plus, everyone, it seemed, pulled behind them an airline-approved, maximum-weight carry-on bag, ignorant of the goings on around them, as they talked on their phones. Looking out at the stark beauty of the mountains in the distance, I figured an archenemy could parachute an invasion force down from the sky, and nobody would notice.

I was in a morose mood, and I had been trying to talk myself out of it all morning. It had started the night before as I was packing for the trip and thinking about Alex's death.

I had called Steve in February to find out if he had heard anything on the recovery of the body. As I had suspected, it had been easily found after the first of the year, when there had been a break in the storms. He had been identified, and the body was shipped back to Tampa, where Steve had his remains cremated. The ashes, in a gallon-sized Ziplock bag, were tucked away in Steve's suitcase.

When I had read the article on the avalanche that killed him, I had just assumed that the other person who died had just been another skier in the group. Steve told me it had been Alex's son, Christian Fairbanks.

Two years earlier, Alex had found out he had a son when he contacted Alicia via Cosmos, an app which connected you to others, allowing you to share pictures and comments. They had arranged to meet up, Alex going to the Swiss Alps, where she lived, to spend some time skiing and getting reacquainted. She had told him about Christian, who had an ex-wife and two young children, and lived in London. He had met his son, and from everything Steve knew, they had instantly hit it off, both of them being avid skiers.

I couldn't imagine the heartbreak and suffering caused by Christian's death, especially for his mother and his two young sons. Apparently neither his mother nor Christian's ex-wife blamed Alex, since Christian had picked the place where they had met up to ski. It had been a favorite of his. Steve had also told me that Alicia did not want Alex's money, and the money would go to Christian's sons.

This turn of events changed my initial feelings about Alex's death. Now instead of being the way he would have chosen to die, given a choice, it had become a tragedy. The fact that he and his son now lived on after death through the boys was a small consolation. I didn't ask Steve how much money Alex had when he died but I hoped it was enough that his grandsons could benefit from their inheritance.

Death was something that I had always been aware of, beginning with my grandparents deaths, my father's mother and father, two months apart, when I was five years old. The grief surrounding those deaths was etched deep into my memory. I had now lived through the deaths of both my parents and all of my aunts and uncles, and now, friends my own age were beginning to die. I had always accepted death's inevitability. But it was still the end, and I had always hated endings and good-byes.

Alex's death brought into focus, once again, the truth that

everything ends. Death didn't hold any joy for me like it did for Cora and Lizzy, who were steady churchgoing Christians. They seemed to have swallowed the Christian religion hook, line, and sinker. And although I had always thought of myself as an optimist, looking at life as if it were a half-full glass and not a half-empty one, it was difficult to be an optimist about death when I believed it was the end of everything. I shook my head, trying to clear out the dark thoughts.

Steve had set up with the National Park Service to spread Alex's ashes in Grand Teton National Park the following day. Evidently, it was not unusual for people to request that their ashes be spread in national parks, and there was a process for getting a permit. The permit for this park prohibited the spreading of the ashes near the lakes at the base of the mountains and in high-traffic areas. Steve had decided to schedule the event in early April, before the place became a crowded vacation destination.

When I had last talked to him, he confirmed everything was set, and he had been in touch with some of his and Alex's mutual friends in the Marine Corps. And, he had gotten in touch with many of the men Alex had trained and competed with during his years of entering triathlons all over the country, including the Iron Man in Hawaii. Also, he'd sent out word of the memorial's date, place, and time over Alex's Cosmos page, before closing the account. "I have no idea who will show up," Steve told me. "Who knows? It could just be you, me, and Simon."

Simon Browne had been a colonel stationed at MARCENT when I was there. He had, upon retiring, along with Alex and Steve, worked for Ziberon, a contracting firm with a stable of former military experts, used by the US military to fill needs for special projects. Like Steve, Simon lived in Tampa, and they both attended the small Marine Corps birthday dinner held there every year on November 10.

So, I was not surprised when I saw them both coming through the arrivals gate. I waved them over. Steve looked tired and older than the last time I had seen him, over two years ago. He reached me first, giving me a smile and a strong hug. Simon stood behind Steve, a grin on his face.

Simon's face was tanned and unlined, except for some small and attractive lines around his eyes. His hair was silver, but he was still fit-looking. In tasseled loafers, pressed khakis, a white button-down shirt with the sleeves rolled up to his elbows, and a navy sweater tied around his neck, he looked like he was on his way to the country club for lunch.

—Life looks like it has been good to you, I said to him.

—You as well, Jules, he said, as his eyes looked me up and down, his polished British accent unchanged from when I had last heard him speak over fifteen years earlier. But, your fashion statement could use some work. He looked pointedly at my feet. I was wearing black-and-white Converse tennis shoes.

I laughed.

—Simon, you were always the charmer. I gave him a light hug. And, it's not a matter of fashion. They're comfortable, and they don't pinch my feet, swollen from the flight.

—You smell the same, he said, still grinning. You still wear the same perfume?

—I do, at least for this trip. It's Bulgari, Au Thé Vert. I haven't worn perfume in years, but this is what I wore in Bahrain, and I decided it was appropriate. I turned to Steve. Any updates since we last talked?

As the three of us headed toward the exit, he told me about a wake that a group of the guys whom Alex trained with and competed against in triathlons had planned for later that evening. The invitation was extended to anybody who had known Alex.

—It's at a place right here in Jackson, called the Million

Dollar Cowboy Bar.

—Nice place? asked Simon.

I looked back and forth between them. Evidently they had not talked about this update on their flight from Tampa. I thought that some things never changed, remembering that the two of them had not seemed to share much information when Simon was the chief of staff of MARCENT in Bahrain, and Steve was the chief of staff at MARCENT's cell at CENTCOM in Tampa. I had thought of them as the Odd Couple. Steve had always been the practical, guy-next-door type of leader, while Simon had been the opposite. In his way of thinking, the rank structure of the military not only demanded obeisance, but permitted people of higher rank greater privileges. Those privileges encompassed many things, including, for Simon, the best of what was available.

—It's reputed to be the best bar in the West, said Steve, looking over at Simon with a look that conveyed the thought: *Really? This is what you care about?*

—The best bar in the West, said Simon, musing. You know, this is the first time I have ever been to Wyoming.

—Me, too, and from what I've read, it's now a variation on the theme of itself, I said.

They both looked at me.

—I will tell you all about my theory after we get checked into our rooms and get something to eat. I haven't had anything but coffee today and I'm starved.

—I look forward to hearing another theory of yours, said Simon, smiling at me. Steve looked at me, confused.

—Right before you came to Bahrain, I said, Simon, Alex, and I went out to eat at the British Club, and after I had too much wine, I regaled them with one of my "variation on a theme" theories.

—I'm sorry I missed that, said Steve, looking at me with a

hint of a smile. But what is a "variation on a theme theory"?

—I believe that everything that happens in life is just a variation on a theme. Meaning that, as things change over time, the changes are just a variation on the themes of life that have existed since humans began walking the earth.

—I don't remember what your theory was about either. All I remember is that it was entertaining, Simon said.

He called for an Uber, and we headed to the hotel at the base of the Tetons. It was a lovely place, chosen by Steve as somewhere not only comfortable but also close to where we would spread Alex's ashes.

After I showered, I put on the somber clothes I had chosen for this trip: a black-and-white knit dress, black leggings, and my ever faithful Converse tennis shoes. I stood in front of the full length mirror, getting ready to practice my theory. I suddenly remembered standing in front of a full-length mirror in the Le Méridien hotel in Bahrain. I had been giving myself a final warning that what I was getting ready to do, go to bed with Alex for the first time, was going to take me to a place that there was no turning back from. I remembered saying to my reflection, "Julia Anne, I sure hope you know what you're doing." I realized that I had no idea where my actions would lead. I didn't stop to consider any of the potential consequences. All I knew at the time was that I physically wanted him so much that I felt like I was vibrating.

I shook my head. *Stop it.* That was a long time ago. I started over again, practicing what I was going to say tonight. I didn't want to be unable to call up the nouns I needed to use to express myself. I knew the days of impromptu speech were gone forever, but I consoled myself with the thought that at least this time I would be sober. But, my heart wasn't in it. That vision of myself at the start of my affair with Alex was stuck in the forefront of my mind.

I went down to the restaurant in the hotel to join Steve and Simon for dinner. They were at the bar, having a drink. Climbing up on the bar stool next to Steve, I got the bartender's attention and ordered two fingers of the local bourbon, Wyoming Whiskey. I raised my glass.

—To Alex. I downed all of it in a single gulp, gasping after I had swallowed it. Their faces said, *What the fuck?* That's all I'm going to have, I said, as they stared at me. But I had to do it. I can't toast a deceased person by just drinking a Coke.

—I'm relieved, said Steve. —It looked for a second like you were preparing to tie one on.

—No, a Coke wouldn't have set quite the same tone, Simon said, with narrowed eyes. He looked at me hard, saying, Jules, I admit it. I don't understand why you came.

—Why did *you* come? I answered back.

—Alex and I worked together closely at MARCENT, every day for months, and we worked together occasionally at Ziberon, always going out to eat after work. When Steve asked me if I wanted to come with him, my calendar was clear.

The bartender came over to see if I wanted another drink.

—Water please, a double with ice. He smiled at me, and went to get the water. I looked at Steve, then at Simon. Alex and I were lovers. I met him my first day in Bahrain. He was then the OIC of the Marine Corps Coordination Element, just arrived from the Naval War College, having no idea of the events unfolding around us. Probably he and I would have rarely seen each other again, but when he became the G-3 of MARCENT, everything changed. I'm here because I loved him. *There,* I thought, *I said it out loud, and to Simon Browne, no less.*

He looked over at Steve.

—You knew this?

Steve nodded.

—She told me when I called her about Alex's death.

—I'm not going to talk about it, I said. It was a long time ago, but he was important to me at one time, and I told Steve I wanted to come when he spread Alex's ashes.

—Fair enough, Simon said. He addressed the bartender, pointing first to himself and then to Steve. Bring us what she just had.

The bartender brought their drinks, and we all raised our glasses.

—To Alex, Simon said. Steve and I lent our voices to the salute, and when Simon had finished his drink, he sat there, shaking his head. Damn. I wonder what else I didn't know about.

I shrugged, smiling.

After we had ordered, Simon looked over at me.

—You were going to enlighten us on . . . what was it again?

—My Wyoming variation on a theme theory, I said, putting down the delicious-looking sourdough roll I had just been getting ready to bite into and sitting up straight in my chair like I had been called upon in a classroom. But, please understand that this theory isn't fully formed yet. I only started constructing it as I read about this area in preparation for the trip, adding to it when I landed here this afternoon and took in the people and the look of the place.

He didn't say anything else but waited on me to continue.

—I'm curious to see what I've missed, Steve said. I don't believe I've ever heard you wax eloquent before.

—Well, I said, smiling at Steve's remark, upon first glance, Wyoming looks starkly untouched by progress. But, when you look closer, you see how it's just a pale reflection of its former self. Still breathtakingly beautiful, but it's natural beauty has been overlaid with human wealth. Did you know that Wyoming has the highest income per capita of any other state? Especially Jackson Hole. I raised my hand, indicating the area around us, like I was Vanna White on the *Wheel of Fortune*. Simon and Steve were looking at me, amused. The last time I had done this, Alex had been sitting there with me. And for an instant, I saw him there, watching me, amused too. I'm sorry, I said, pushing back my chair and abruptly standing. I can't do this. I hurried out of the restaurant, headed for my room.

Grief incarnate claimed me, my body and emotions ganging up against my mind to express unmitigated grief, a reaction that I didn't expect, and I couldn't control it. Tears rolled down my cheeks; my breathing was rapid; and by the time I reached my room, I was sobbing in great gasps. I tried to make it stop, but I couldn't. My body was following the lead of my emotions, not my mind.

I kicked off my shoes and tore off my clothes, leaving them on the floor. I was, all of a sudden, so cold. I turned on the warm water, filling the bathtub. Sinking down into the tub, my mental jukebox started playing Bonnie Raitt's iconic song of unrequited love, "I Can't Make You Love Me."

Alex had never loved me, but that was something I had never wanted to admit to myself. It hit me in the face with the full force of its truth. He had liked me well enough, was even fond of me, and he had desired my body with an enveloping passion, which had become my addiction. But I had never touched his soul. I don't know how long I sat there, sobbing. It seemed like I cried for everything and everyone I had lost in my life. When I became aware that the water in the tub was cold, I got out and wrapped a towel around me. I made myself brush my teeth, get dressed for bed, and pick my clothes up off the floor.

I was watching the Food Network, something to keep my mind in a safe place before I fell asleep, when I heard a knocking at my door.

—Jules, it's Steve.

I went to the door, opening it for him to come in.

—I was just checking on you before Simon and I drop in for a while on Alex's wake.

When I looked up into his face, the tears started again.

—I'm sorry, I said. It just happened. I'm sorry, I said again, unable to stop the tears. He was my hero. I need to pull myself together tonight. I don't want to be a wreck tomorrow when we go up on the mountain.

Steve's eyes were full of tears, his face lined with sorrow.

—I'm sorry. I don't mean for us to have a tear fest. He smiled.

—I miss him, he said. It's not that I really saw him anymore after we both retired from Ziberon. Jo and I bought that vacation home in California near our youngest daughter and her husband, and we've been spending a good part of the year out there, enjoying our grandsons, spoiling them like grandparents are supposed to, right? Alex was involved with his triathlons. Now I find out he had a son, who died in the same tragic way he did.

—You know, I said, he did tell me about Alicia, but called her Alice. I don't know why I didn't think of her when you told me he left his estate to Alicia and Christian Fairbanks. Anyway, I picked up on the fact she was special to him, someone who he met when he was in college at the American University in Paris. I remember him telling me that he almost married her, but that he didn't want to be married. He sounded like an alcoholic at an AA meeting, hitting the highlights of his addiction. You know what I mean? But, I think he was just kidding himself. Of course, little did he know that she had his child.

—I didn't know he met her in college. I wondered how they met, but I didn't feel like it was my place to ask her.

—She was the one, I said. I'm just glad he met up with her again and found out about his son. It makes me too sad to think his last thoughts could have been for his son's life. I like to tell myself he didn't have time to think too much. So . . . you two are on your way to the wake, then?

—I feel like I have to, he said. But I won't stay long. And, I doubt Simon will either. He talks a big game, but he's an old man, too.

—I won't tell him you said that. And, I've heard it said that sixty is the new fifty. If you think about it that way, he's got a few more years before he enters old man territory. Steve, you're not old, either. All right?

He nodded at me and opened the door, saying,

—We can meet in the morning downstairs at nine.

—Sounds like a plan, I said, and closed the door after him.

---

The next morning, I made sure I was downstairs early and dressed for the cold: a calf-length black wool coat, and a Fair Isle–patterned scarf. I looked exactly how I felt, sad and heartsick. When I had checked my appearance before I left my room, the skin around my eyes was puffy from my cry-a-thon the night before, and my eyes reflected heartbreak. I thought that my age accentuated the look of grief.

Steve showed up before nine in a dark-brown wool coat, his face mirroring mine. As he joined me, I found myself smiling at him.

—Well . . . how was the wake?

—I'm not a good judge, he said, shrugging. I'd never been to that type of wake before. A bunch of guys with a good excuse to drink. We didn't stay long. Just walked around, met everyone there. They're coming this morning, at least they said so last night. I guess we'll see.

He looked at his watch, then in the direction of the elevator. There was no sign of Simon.

—He'll be here exactly at nine, I said, seeing his look of concern. If he hasn't changed, he'll want to make a grand entrance, strolling in right on the dot. He was never one to be late.

Just as I finished speaking, the elevator doors opened, and Simon walked out, looking well-groomed in his dark-gray wool coat and black scarf. I looked at my watch. Nine o'clock. I grinned at Steve. His face broke into a smile as he nodded at me.

—Good morning, I said, as Simon joined us. I apologize for last night. My body decided to follow the lead of my emotions, but I'm good now. How was the wake?

—Very American, he said. No singing.

—Singing? Steve and I said, in tandem.

Simon looked at us, shaking his head as if he were thinking, *Poor Americans. They can't even hold a proper wake.*

—Oh, that's right! I said. Don't the British sing at wakes? It's charming.

—Charming? Simon said.

—Not charming like "Mary had a little lamb; his fleece was white as snow" charming. But, a charming bond of solidarity that transcends the ordinary.

—Exactly, he said, nodding his approval.

Steve looked back and forth between us and shook his head.

—Let's do this, he said.

Making the way up the mountain road, the driver of the Uber kept to the posted speed limit of twenty-five miles per hour. The road was lightly snow-covered, and the sky was gray and thick with clouds. The rational part of my brain didn't want it to snow, thinking it would be easier getting off the mountain if it didn't. But part of me thought that the beauty of a snow-filled sky would be the perfect backdrop against which to scatter Alex's ashes as they mixed with the snowflakes in the air.

We arrived at the designated spot about fifteen minutes before the send-off. That's what I had decided to call it. There wasn't going to be a ceremony of any sort. Steve was going to say a few words, and then each of us that wanted to could take a handful of Alex's ashes and release them over the edge of the lookout. As we walked over to where everyone was standing, I counted twenty-four people. I didn't recognize anyone. We joined the group, standing close together for warmth.

With the mountain wind, it was easily close to freezing, feeling even colder since the clouds were thick, threatening snow. I looked out at the view, not really listening to Steve's words. It was a glorious vista, isolated-looking and untouched by progress. My thoughts were interrupted by a man who whispered close to my ear.

—You could get lost out there.

I turned to look at him. About my age, he looked like a modern-day pirate. A little over six feet tall, he was slim, dressed in a black leather jacket and jeans, looking like if you touched him, he would be all hard muscle. He had a full head of dark hair, streaked with silver, and it was pulled back into a pony tail. He had a small silver loop in his left ear; his square face was clean-shaven; and when I looked into his eyes, I saw a gray-blue like the clouds in the sky above us, arresting against his dark skin.

I met his gaze for a few seconds and then turned back around to see Steve taking out the bag of ashes and opening it. He invited everyone there to take a handful, say a few words, and release Alex's ashes into the air. We all took turns dipping a hand into the bag. Some people said nothing, just opening their hands and allowing the ashes to blow away. The people who said something said it softly, like a prayer, and I couldn't make out their words. I watched as the pirate took some; walked out to the very edge of the overlook; and leveling his head with his palm, blew on them. They spread in a cloud and were soon gone from sight.

I took my cue from Steve, walked over to the edge, and closed my eyes. *Thank you, Alex, for coming into my life. You were the best and the worst thing that has ever happened to me. And, if I had to do it all over again, I would do it without a moment's hesitation.* I reluctantly opened my hand. The ashes, caught in an uptake of wind, started swirling overhead. I watched them as they disappeared.

Once everyone who took ashes had released them, Steve emptied out the bag, shaking the remaining ashes off the edge of the overlook. Steve walked back over to stand with me and Simon. A few of the others came up to talk to him before they left. The pirate also came over and introduced himself as Darius Lawson. I listened as he said he had been a friend of Alex's. They had gone to college together and had joined the Marine Corps together. At that, I raised my head to look at him as he talked. He noticed and turned to look into my eyes for a heartbeat before returning his attention to Steve.

He said that after they graduated, they realized that their education to that point had been a combination of well-rounded liberal studies and the pleasures of Paris, and it had not prepared them for jobs in the real world. Here he laughed—a carefree laugh, which sounded strange under the circumstances.

—We were absolutely fucking clueless about the demands of the real world, he said.

He explained that both of them had been good athletes, involved in skiing, paragliding, and running. It had been his idea that they both should join the Marine Corps. The adventurous glamour of the Corps had an appeal, plus they had both needed jobs. As it turned out, Darius didn't stay beyond his first tour, saying,

—I was an infantry officer, too. But the rules of the military, that is, always being on a tight string, always accountable to someone with a higher rank, and not being able to go where I wanted when I wanted made me realize that the Corps was not for me.

He said that after he had moved on to working as a mountain guide in Canada, they had taken vacations together every summer for years, in the Alps, to paraglide.

I suddenly remembered that Alex had mentioned Darius but not by name. We were in a period of waiting before the start of the war, and Alex had taken the weekend away from the camp. He pulled out his slides and gave me a surprise slide show of scenes from his life going back ten or more years. The slides of Alex and Darius were not closeup shots, but Alex had said the person with him was his oldest friend, telling me that they used to go to the Alps together every summer to paraglide.

Darius said he had eventually taken a job with a hiking outfitter, working out of Australia, and Alex's work had become more demanding, so their trips together stopped. But, they had kept up with each other over the years.

—He was like my twin brother. When I read your post on his Cosmos page about how he died, I knew I had to be here.

While he talked, I stood there listening and watched the ashes making their way to wherever the wind would take them. My mind had already turned toward the prospect of going home. Steve and Simon weren't going back to Tampa until the following day, something about the cost of the flight plus the hotel being cheaper if they stayed an additional night. I didn't really understand how that worked, but was just relieved I wouldn't be sitting in the airport with them, waiting on our flights. I hated conversations where no information of any significance is exchanged, just babble to fill the empty space. And, it was over. I wanted to go home.

---

I arrived at the airport about an hour and a half before my flight. While I was sitting at the departure gate, I played backgammon on my phone. Since Lizzy had introduced me to the game app earlier in the year, I had become addicted, playing a couple of games every night before bedtime as a way to wind down. Now I wanted to wind down from my trip and clear my mind of everything but the game. A person sat down in the seat beside me, and I looked up and did a double take. It was the pirate, Darius Lawson.

—Are you going to Orlando, too? I said.

—Nope, he said, shaking his head. Denver. He pointed to the gate across from where we were sitting. But, I saw you sitting here, recognized you, and realized that I didn't introduce myself to you this morning. I'm Darius, Darius Lawson. And your name is?

—Jules, I said, realizing I had not said a single word to him when we were up on the mountain. Jules Walker. I knew Alex in Bahrain. He was a colonel then. The G-3 at MARCENT. I was a lieutenant colonel. One of the two staff judge advocates.

—You're a Marine? And a lawyer? He looked surprised and there was interest in his eyes.

—Yes. Or, at least, I used to be. I'm not a lawyer anymore. I resigned from the bar when I retired from the military.

—I never had any dealings with a lawyer when I was in the Corps, he said, the expression on his face still interested, but now his eyes held something else. When Alex was the G-3 at MARCENT, did he work with his lawyers a lot?

—No, not really, I said. Like most Marines, he didn't like dealing with lawyers. I can only remember one time when we were asked to weigh in on what he was doing. It had to do with the US military's involvement in Djibouti.

—Why did you come, then? he said, looking confused. Then his expression cleared. You and Alex were lovers?

—Bingo! I said, impressed. I bet you're good at party games like Twenty Questions. He grinned at me, his eyes crinkling around the edges, the mirth in them appearing out of nowhere.

But, I said, he was more than just a good time. I actually loved him.

—I'm sorry, he said, while not looking sorry at all. It's none of my business. I'm too curious for my own good. He never stayed with any one very long, except Alice. You know about her? I nodded.

—He told me about her.

—He did?

—Yes, he did. But, I should tell you that I was married when I knew Alex. I think the secretive nature of our relationship plus the fact we were in a bubble in Bahrain, with war imminent, had something to do with why he told me about her. Anyway, he made it sound like she was just someone he knew when he was young, in college, and he decided he didn't want to be tied down. But, when Steve told me he left everything to her and his son, Christian, I figured there was more to the story than he let on.

—Yeah, he said, the mirth in his eyes gone now. She broke his heart, or at least that was my take on it. She was a beauty, and maybe she still is. Tall and willowy, with long dark hair. An artist, she calls herself. Her parents were wealthy. British expats who lived in Switzerland. It made perfect sense that's where she was living when Alex met up with her. He was excited to find out about his son. I guess it was too far for his son to come just to spread his ashes.

—You don't know then? I said, searching his face.

—Know what?

I told him everything I knew about the skiing accident with Christian.

—When Steve first told me about Alex's death, I thought he had died only doing what he loved, skiing, I said. But then when Steve located Alicia Fairbanks, he found out about the tragedy of their son's death.

—All I knew is what Steve posted on Alex's Cosmos page, said Darius, looking solemn.

—I didn't see Steve's post. But Steve wouldn't have wanted to make him out as a tragic figure.

—Yeah, that makes sense, he said, nodding his head. I expected him to make his good-byes and get up to leave, but he didn't move.

—You live in Orlando? he said.

—No. I live about two hours north of there, in the center of the northern part of the state, a one-traffic-light town called Melrose. My definition of heaven.

—I've never been to Florida.

—Right, I said, smiling at him. No mountains. Where do you call home?

—Colorado, right now. Telluride.

—Do tell. I understand it's beautiful there.

I listened as he told me about the breathtaking San Juan Mountains. He sounded like Alex talking about the mountains, like they were idols he worshiped.

—You told Steve that you and Alex were twins. Did you mean your love of snow-covered places?

—You were listening, he said, smiling a beautiful smile, his teeth looking so white against his dark skin. Yeah, he and I were bound together by our love of the mountains, and we both wanted to experience what the world had to offer. He always felt like the brother I never had.

—Then, I take it, you're a searcher, too? Still haven't found what you're looking for? Or have you found it, and it's not what you thought it would be. I said it without thinking.

—God! he said, his face pulling back like I had punched him. You're direct, aren't you?

—I used to be, but not so much anymore, I said. As you may

remember, in the Marine Corps you have to cut to the chase. There's no beating about the bush on issues. That's one thing I miss about it. And, I have some of the searcher in me too, so I can spot that characteristic when I see it.

He nodded.

—I guess you could label me a searcher, he said, and I'm still searching. But, don't ask me what for, because I can't really say. Maybe I'll recognize it when I find it, or maybe it's all about the freedom of the search. I don't know. My eyebrows must have been raised at his words. What? he said.

—Nothing. I was just listening. I guess I didn't expect an answer. You seem to know yourself. No bullshit. It's nice.

—Is that one of the things Alex liked about you, he said, smiling at me, your candidness?

—I have no idea. He never said. And, it was another lifetime ago. But . . . well . . . frankly, for him, I have to believe it was mostly about the sex. In my memory, with my love of Alex, I see it now as mind-blowing sex.

—I can see that, he said, staring me down. But, not literally. I'm not looking! He laughed and I smiled, shaking my head.

—Can I ask you something? I said.

—Sure, he said, sitting there like he was prepared to take a physical punch.

—Would you consider yourself a "bad boy?" You sort of look like it, what with your earring, your long hair, and your hard-looking body. And the little you told Steve about your vagabond life; it would make sense.

—Vagabond life? he said. He looked down at himself and then back at me. Hard-looking body? Bad boy? No. I don't have the right attitude. I'm not much of a rule breaker. I work out because it's a lifelong habit; I keep my hair long because it's easier than getting it cut; the earring is my personal reminder that I chose not to live a normal life . . . Vagabond. That's a good word.

—I admire your ability to live like that, I said.

—You do?

—Yes, I do. It's easy to live a normal life but not so easy to take the uncharted path. Since you have piqued my interest, do you mind telling me how you ended up going to the American University in Paris?

—Piqued your interest, huh? He seemed to be thoroughly enjoying our talk. Well, my parents divorced when I was fourteen. My dad was American, and my mother was French. After the divorce, my mother and I traveled to Paris to see her family. I fell in love with France. I decided I wanted to go to college there.

—Did you grow up speaking French?

—Sure did. With my mother. Je ne la parle plus beaucoup.

—Lucky you. A speaker of French, even though you don't speak it much anymore. You must be a real heartbreaker.

—You understand French?

—Only a little, I said. I took French in high school and a conversational course in college, but the only time I've ever used it was when I visited Paris ages ago.

We both looked up, as a woman began the announcement that boarding was about to begin for my flight. Then we looked at each other. I smiled and stood up, and he stood as well, looking down at me. I stuck out my hand.

—It was nice meeting and talking to you, Darius Lawson.

He took my outstretched hand. His hand was large and warm, and his handshake was firm; the shock traveled all the way up my arm. I went to pull my hand away, but he held on to it, like it was a life-line, looking at me. Then he let it go.

—You too, Jules Walker, he said, looking into my eyes. Then he raised his hand, turned, and walked away.

My fingers were tingling with the feel of his touch as I watched his back for a few seconds before I turned to go get in line to board the plane. It was half empty. I guessed not many people went from Jackson to Orlando in the middle of the week in early April. I thought about what Darius had told me as I found my seat. I was struck by the fact that Alex's friend was named Darius. I thought I remembered that someone named Darius had been the Persian ruler defeated by Alexander the Great. With this new pairing of Alexander and Darius, Darius was the one left standing.

I got settled in my window seat, looking out at the Wyoming evening sky, and sat there, rubbing my hand. I had never been one to read romance novels, but I imagined something like this, this jolt of electric shock, would be one of the givens in such a novel. I had thought this would never happen to me again. I wondered why my body responded to him in the way it had responded to Alex. He was physically beautiful, seemed intelligent, and lived a nomadic life. Because he was like Alex in those ways, maybe I was drawn to him. *It doesn't matter, though*, I thought. *I'll never see him again.*

My mental jukebox was playing, softly in the background and I listened to what it had decided to play. It was "Don't Let the Sun Go Down on Me." *Damn it!* I muttered. I got up to get out my carry-on out of the over-head bin, and dug into it to get my iPad. I had downloaded a couple of movies on it, and I really needed to drown out that music. I started watching *Avatar*, my favorite movie of all time. It didn't hurt that the hero was a former Marine, and the love story was a central part of the epic story line. Before long, I had forgotten about the song, immersed in the world of Pandora.

# Brace Yourself

On a morning in early June, my mental jukebox was playing Howie Day as background noise, in a nonstop loop. I had become accustomed to this random playing of music, often loudly but sometimes so softly that some days I hardly noticed it. This morning, though, "Brace Yourself" was crowding my mind, especially whenever I wasn't concentrating on a task, like reading the morning news. I couldn't see how it was relevant to anything in particular, because it was sort of a love song, and it had a rhythm and emotion that made one feel on the precipice of something extraordinary.

That morning, I shrugged it off, deciding that my mind was just in a good mood. For one thing, the lakefront was beginning to look amazing. A small patch of the beautiful, purple pickerelweed had begun to get a foothold. It had happened after I got back from Wyoming, in the spring push for regeneration and growth. And, the shoreline in front of my house was entirely clear of the evil torpedo grass. In May, Josh had suggested that we should use their boat to remove the grass in the water that was over my head before the summer was upon us. I tossed out the weed razor, and we allowed it to sink to the bottom. Then, he inched the boat along while I held on to the tool for dear life, with thick, well-padded work gloves. His idea worked like a charm. It took a month of weekends to clear out the grass, but at the end of each day that we worked on it, all of that cut grass floating on the surface of the water was a truly wonderful sight.

Another welcome development was the reappearance of saw grass, the water plant that had defined the lake when I was a girl. In the fall, Lizzy had noticed it back in the cove. We had thought its reappearance was an anomaly, having survived back there because it was in a part of the lake that was undisturbed by boats and people. But then, in spring, we began to see it all over the lake. I didn't understand why it was coming back, although it could have had something to do with all of the rainfall the area experienced during Hurricane Irma, two years earlier. The flourishing of the saw grass was a happy homecoming, something I felt signaled the good health of the lake.

And, I had a new family member on the lake. Unbeknownst to me or Lizzy, Cora had put her property up for sale on Lake George after Christmas. This event coincided with a for sale sign on the property next door to the one my parents had owned. Cora, her daughter, and her son-in-law had gone in together to buy it. The house had been neglected for years and it needed a lot of work to even make it livable, but it was on a large lot, with a magnificent view of the entire lake.

Telling me about the house after she had bought it, Cora was, for once, completely honest and open with me, saying, "I knew after I had spent some time at your place, I couldn't be truly happy with a lake house unless it was on this lake." She didn't say that purchasing the property gave her a feeling of peace, but I suspected it did. And there was no talk of building a cracker house. Perhaps, at some point, she would revisit that idea, but she had plenty of projects to keep her occupied.

Since her grandkids were getting old enough to learn how to

ski and wakeboard, she wanted them to experience what she had experienced growing up on the lake. Another secret she had kept was that, after Daddy's funeral, she had paid Helen for Daddy's old turquoise-and-white Redfish, a 1950s runabout. She had it trailered from his garage and placed it in a climate-controlled storage facility. She had announced this fact to me, saying, "I'm sending it off to South Carolina to have it completely restored so that I can use it to teach Evey and Cal to ski." I didn't say anything about the fact that Evey didn't seem like she would be interested in learning to ski, because she didn't like the outdoors, preferring to stay inside with a book, or that Cal seemed more the type for skateboarding or speed racing with his mountain bike.

But I was thrilled with Cora's news, and I had no reason to think Lizzy wasn't going to be thrilled, as well. Cora would have to learn how to operate the boat, since Lizzy had been the only one who had learned to drive it, but I figured that was something she and Lizzy could work out between them. In the meantime, Cora had contracted to have the existing garage on her property enlarged so that it could easily accommodate the boat; she had a boat ramp poured so that it would be an easy task to take the boat in and out of the water; and she had a covered two-story dock built, where she could sit and view the wide expanse of the lake. Once Cora got hold of a project, there was no stopping her. Her purchase of the lake property and her plans to restore Daddy's old Redfish made me think that, perhaps, Grace had decided to touch Cora's life, too.

Lizzy and Josh had kept up their practice of coming to visit me at the lake pretty much every weekend. I knew that would change now that Sammy had given birth to her twin girls, but it would always be here for them. She and Josh regularly spent time out on the lake, fishing. Lizzy no longer was keen to catch fish to eat but was at a point in her fish-catching life where she preferred to catch and release. They had taken to inviting their friends to the lake for weekend days of sunbathing, swimming, and socializing. In thinking about these things, I felt that Grace had touched Lizzy, as well.

---

That afternoon, after mowing my yard, I went into the house to get some water to drink while I cooled down. Coming in the door off the porch, I stopped at the bulletin board I kept there with photos of lake life, then and now. Along with the pictures, I had tacked up a Chinese fortune, taken from one of the many fortune cookies Josh and Lizzy and I had eaten because of Josh's love of the local Chinese takeout restaurant:

Doing what you love is freedom.
Loving what you do is happiness.

Just as every other time I looked at it there, I wasn't really sure it was true, given all the variables impacting a person at any given time in life, but it was a positive thought to keep in mind.

I decided to go for a quick swim to cool off. As I was changing out of my work clothes, I heard a knock on my front door. Hapa started barking and HB joined in. I called out,

—Wait just a minute! I'm coming!

Not wanting to take the chance of the girls getting out, I walked through to the carport, seeing a car behind my truck, one I didn't recognize. I came out into the yard to see Darius at the front door.

—Darius? What the fuck?

He smiled and walked toward me. He looked the same: his hair pulled back into a pony tail, his earring glinting in the sun, but instead of a leather jacket and jeans, he wore a white T-shirt with "Explore Australia" on the front and blue hiking shorts.

—Jules! he said, You didn't get my text?

I hadn't checked my phone when I came in from mowing and told him so.

—How did you get my number or, come to think of it, know where I live?

He looked around him at the freshly mown grass, nodding.

—I just looked you up on the White pages website. You were easy to find. In my text, I said I was on my way and would be here about, he looked at his Apple Watch, well, about now.

With him standing right in front of me, I had the urge to reach out and touch him, to make sure he was really there. I studied him, standing there in my swimming shorts, long-sleeved UV rash guard, and flip-flops. I looked up into his eyes.

—I was just going to go in the water to cool off. You want to join me? I pointed to the shorts he was wearing. They'll dry off in no time, or we can put them in the dryer. I think my brother-in-law has some shorts here you can wear while they dry.

—Why not? he said, looking like he was making up his mind about something having nothing to do with going for a dip in the lake. He bent down and lightly kissed me on the lips as we looked into each other's eyes. It felt like the most natural thing in the world for him to do.

—It's good to see you, Jules.

—You, too, Darius, I said, reaching up to pull his face back down to mine. I needed to feel his lips again. They were amazingly soft. It had been so long since I had kissed anyone on the lips that I had completely forgotten what it felt like. It felt intimate. The biblical proverb, "An honest answer is like a kiss on the lips," came to me from the reaches of my memory. And that's what the kiss felt like, an honest answer. *But, what is the question*, I thought.

I motioned him to come with me, and he put his arm around

my shoulders, like it was something he did every day. We walked around the carport, the lake coming into view.

—Wow! he said. This is a beautiful place.

—Yes it is. How do you find yourself here . . . in Florida?

As we walked down to the lake, the cool breeze in our faces, he told me about the adventure company in Tampa he had taken a job with.

—Understand, I'm their Colorado guy. I flew in yesterday, and I'll get together with the owners and others, like me, tomorrow. But Jules, he said, looking serious, you're going to think this sounds weird, and I swear, I'm not crazy, but when you held my hand at the airport, I felt this jolt of electricity. That's really what it was like. I've never felt anything like it before.

—Really? I felt it, too.

—You did? he said, searching my eyes. Have you ever experienced anything like that before?

—Yes, once before . . . Alex.

He nodded and looked out at the lake. The wind was ruffling the surface of the lake, the water sparkling, reflecting the sunlight off the water. Looking back at me, he said

—I'm not Alex.

—I know you're not. You seem intelligent like he was; you're physically beautiful like he was; your lifestyle makes you seem a free spirit, as he was. And maybe you're fearless like he was. But, you're easy to talk to. He wasn't. You strike me as open, like a window thrown open on a beautiful spring day. Maybe it's because you seem like a happy person. He wasn't. And, you felt that jolt, too. He didn't.

I stood there looking at him, and he grinned.

—A beautiful spring day? Jules, you're full of shit.

—No, Darius, I'm not. That's the way I see it. I shrugged my shoulders.

He didn't say anything else. I watched him as he pulled his T-shirt off over his head. His torso was triangular, his shoulders wide and his waist and hips narrower. The muscles in his hips, shoulders, and upper body flexed as he slid the shirt off, and I noticed a small tattoo on the right side of his lower abdomen. I squinted to make it out against his dark skin. It was a Marine Corps tattoo, a very small anchor, globe, and eagle. I couldn't make out if semper fidelis was a part of the tattoo, but I suspected it was. *Once a Marine, always a Marine,* I thought. As he bent down to take off his shoes, I went ahead and stepped out of my flip-flops. I walked into the lake, feeling the coolness of the water bubbling up from a nearby spring. He came running past me and dove under the water, splashing me as he took his plunge. He swam underwater for a good ten yards before he surfaced.

—This water feels fantastic! he said.

—It does, I said, as I started swimming toward him.

His face looked radiant. There was nothing unhappy or perturbed in his expression. The French phrase *joie de vivre* came to mind as he embraced the moment with abandon.

As I got close to him, he reached out, and taking my hand, he slowly pulled me to him. He pressed me, weightless in the water, tight up against his body, my legs going around his waist without any conscious thought. Holding me there, he looked into my eyes.

—I didn't have any choice. I had to come, he said.

This time I got lost in his kiss.

—You two need to get a room, a voice said behind me.

I turned my head to see Milt and Conrad hurriedly making their way onto the dock. I spun around to face them, and Darius put his arms around my waist. With his arms around me and the feel of his breath on my neck, it was hard to focus.

—And who is this beautiful man? Milt said.

I smiled at them, saying,

—Milt and Conrad, meet Darius.

—Hi, guys. Nice to meet you, said Darius. I could hear the smile in his voice.

—Yes, it's nice to meet you too, said Milt. I want to know all about you, Darius, but we're running late for practice. He looked at me. I will talk to *you* later. He got onto his boat, and began unmooring the boat from the dock.

—You have some time to think about what you want to tell him, Conrad said, in a stage whisper. He grinned.

He got aboard Milt's boat and Milt quickly backed out from the dock, and turning the boat toward his mother's place, zoomed across the lake, the flag fluttering at the rear of the boat for all it was worth. I turned around to face Darius.

—Milt, the dark-headed one is my neighbor. Conrad, his partner, lives over there. I pointed across the lake. My baby sister has known Milt since they were teenagers, and he's one of the nicest people you'll ever meet. One of those rare types who would give you the shirt off his back if you needed it. But he makes it his business to know everything that's happening on the lake. And you, Darius Lawson, are definitely of interest.

—Is that so? Darius said. He watched the activity across the lake where Milt's boat was headed. What's going on over there?

—Those people belong to the ski club—water ski club. The club travels all over the Southeast in the summer, putting on shows. They have a big event coming up over the Fourth of July weekend, in Palatka, on the St. Johns River.

—Interesting, he said. I didn't know people still water skied. Sounds like something I should try.

—They do, and you should. But, Darius, I need to get something to eat. Are you hungry?

—It's not food I'm hungry for, he said. He kissed me again, long and hard, with an intensity of purpose.

When I pulled away from his kiss, I looked at him, searching his eyes. They looked back at me, steady and unblinking. I couldn't read them.

—Come to think of it, I said, amused, I think we should fuck each other's brains out, and then I'll fix us something to eat.

—Damn straight! he said.

—Listen, Darius, I'm serious.

—So am I, he said.

—Why did you drive all the way here? To see if that jolt of electricity was real? He didn't say anything. If so, we are at the stage of life where we don't have the luxury of time to tiptoe around each other. If you want to find out, we're burning daylight.

He laughed. It was a long belly laugh, that made his eyes look like slits in his face.

—God, Jules! he said, once he could speak. You're a woman after my own heart.

And, he didn't let me go. He took my hand in his as we got out of the water and headed toward the house.

---

Now, Darius and I regularly FaceTime, and we get together throughout the year. When the COVID pandemic hit the world, three years ago, he drove his 1990s Range Rover Defender to Florida to stay with me. Later that year, after we had our vaccinations, he left to go back to Colorado, but that time together, with the outside world kept at bay by the pandemic, was transformational for me. We learned all about each other, and it seemed we talked about most everything that had happened in our lives. It was like we passed, unmentioned, a marker in our relationship, sealing our bond.

The next year, he came to Florida to spend the late spring and early summer with me before his busy fall and winter season of work. Then, last year, I went to Colorado to spend the summer with him after both my dogs died of old age, one month apart, in the early spring. I ended up staying with him for six months.

This coming winter, we are talking about going to northern Canada to spend time together, hoping to see the northern lights. The trip, he says, is to commemorate his retirement from working full time. We'll have to just figure out what works for us. Surprisingly, my sisters have accepted his presence in my life, neither of them weighing in on the not-exactly-traditional nature of our relationship.

I'm also working on making peace with myself, accepting who I am, faults and all. I figure that what time I have left shouldn't be wasted on rehashing past events or thinking about how I could have done something differently. I'm trying to live each day being in the moment, as Kat is fond of saying.

And, in thinking back on the year that changed my life, I find myself thinking about the concept of Grace. I've decided it's often called amazing for a very good reason.

www.ingramcontent.com/pod-product-compliance
Lightning Source LLC
LaVergne TN
LVHW061616070526
838199LV00078B/7302